WILDFIRE

Destruction of the Dead

SHAUN HARBINGER

BOOKS IN THIS SERIES

For all the survivors everywhere.

CHAPTER 1

THE MORNING SUN PEEKED THROUGH the high clouds and cast a cold light over the distant cliffs and beaches. Standing on the deck of *The Big Easy*, the metal of the safety railing cold against my palms and the boat rolling easily on the gentle waves, I felt a heavy dread in the pit of my stomach. I was trying to remember why I had volunteered to distribute the antivirus to the survivors on the mainland.

I should run from the danger that lurked beyond those cliffs, not willingly go toward it. Any sane person would turn the boat's nose out to the open sea and give the engines full throttle until the coastline was nothing more than a bad memory.

If it weren't for the fact that my brother, Joe, and my parents were alive somewhere on the mainland, I wouldn't hesitate to flee to the relative safety of the sea.

But as long as there was a slim hope of finding my family, I couldn't run. I had to fight. I had to risk my life in a land infested with zombies and hybrids until I found the people I loved. Leaving Joe and my parents to their fate was not an option.

A few yards from where I stood, a big seagull dropped into the water with a splash, then took to the air again with a small fish wriggling helplessly in its beak.

I turned away from the sea and distant cliffs and went through the door that led to the boat's living area. Lucy was still asleep in our bedroom below deck so I decided to surprise her with breakfast. After all, today was the day we were due to return to Apocalypse Island. They should have made the first batch of antivirus by now and have it ready for distribution.

I might as well make our final morning pleasurable in some small way, even if that small pleasure was just a plate of hash browns, canned tomatoes, and sausages. For the past three days, we had tried to enjoy ourselves by lounging on the deck, eating meals with Sam and Tanya either on the *Easy* or the *Escape*, and singing along to Survivor Radio.

Listening to the radio was bittersweet; on the one hand it provided us with music and a reminder that there had once been a time that was more carefree. On the other, it reminded me that Johnny Drake was dead, his body ripped apart by Vess at Site Alpha Two.

And although none of us mentioned Apocalypse Island or the job ahead of us, it seemed to hang like an unspoken secret in the air, always present and fast-approaching as the days passed too quickly.

I turned on the radio as I reached the kitchen area. Don Henley was singing about the boys of summer. Taking the hash browns and sausages from the freezer, I sang along. I was way out of tune but didn't care.

The frying pan clattered on top of the stove as I set it down too heavily. Hoping it hadn't woken Lucy because I wanted her to get as much sleep as she could, I then added a little oil and turned up the electric ring beneath the pan.

When the oil was hot, I added the hash browns and sausages. They sizzled in the pan and the smell made my mouth water. There was once a time when I would have cooked this much food just for myself, and then spent the rest of the day sitting in front of the TV watching movies or playing games. I had fought digital zombies in *The Last of Us*, *The Walking Dead*, and *Day Z*. I had "died" many times in the games but there had always been another life, another chance.

Now I was living the harsh reality of what had once been a pleasurable pastime. There was no second chance, no reset button.

The world had gone to hell, or at least this part of it had. According to Sam and Tanya, the virus hadn't reached America. If that was true, and only Britain was affected, I wondered what the rest of the world was planning to do about the situation.

They must know what was happening from satellite images. Those images would show the zombie hordes and the destruction and death they left in their wake. They would also show the military encampments and positions that had been set up by the army as they tried to take control of the chaos.

Would the foreign leaders try to help us, or would they think, *To hell with it* and bombard us with nuclear weapons instead, killing everyone and everything, alive or undead, just to be safe? They couldn't risk the virus reaching their shores. If protecting themselves meant killing innocent people and turning Britain into a nuclear wasteland, I was sure they wouldn't lose much sleep over it.

Lucy appeared at the doorway and waved at me. Her expression and posture as she came into the living area said that she was still sleepy. Her blonde hair was pinned up into a messy bun. She wore the oversized 'Sail To Your Destiny' T-shirt that she sometimes slept in. As she padded barefoot across the carpet to the sofa, she said, "That smells good."

"I thought we should have a good breakfast," I said, "since we don't know when we'll get a chance to eat properly again." I wanted to add, "If ever" but I restrained myself. Lucy knew as well as I did that this could be the last time we both stood here on *The Big Easy*. We had seen too much death to take anything for granted.

4

She nodded and dropped onto the sofa, turning her head away from the morning light streaming in through the windows, her eyes half-closed.

"You okay?" I asked.

"I'm just not a morning person. You know that."

I did. I also knew that she had recently been bitten by a zombie and had been in danger of turning into one of the undead. She'd been injected with the faulty vaccine and then with the new antivirus. It was understandable that she might suffer side effects from that experience.

As if reading my mind, she looked over at me and said, "I'm fine, Alex. Really." She got up and came into the kitchen. "I'll make coffee." She turned on the electric kettle and began to spoon instant coffee and sugar into two mugs.

On the radio, Don faded out to be replaced by 10cc singing "I'm Not In Love".

I sighed and concentrated on the hash browns and sausages sizzling in the pan. Unlike the singers in 10cc, I was finding it difficult to deny my feelings for Lucy.

I had always liked her, and she was the reason I had gone hiking in Wales with Mike and Elena. But my feelings for Lucy then were no more than a powerful physical attraction. Powerful enough to get an out-of-shape gamer-geek like me onto the Welsh mountains, sure, but still only a physical attraction.

We had been through a lot together since the day the zombie apocalypse began and now shared a strong emotional bond. I hadn't realized just how strong until we had been separated. I had risked my life to get a message to Lucy, and then risked it again to get the chemical that was needed for the antivirus that could save her from being turned. And it had all been worth it.

She turned away from the boiling kettle and poked me in the ribs playfully. "Why are you up so early, anyway? You don't like mornings any more than I do."

"Ouch," I said, moving aside to avoid her jabbing finger.

"That did not hurt, Alex."

"It did. Stop poking me and concentrate on making the coffee," I joked.

She raised an eyebrow. "You've been chased by zombies, shot at by the army, and almost eaten by patient zero but you're afraid of my little finger?"

"Yep," I said, nodding and backing away.

She held her index finger in front of my face, a mischievous look in her eyes. "This is what scares the brave Alex Harley?" Lunging forward, she tried to jab me in the ribs again.

I stepped backward quickly, slapping her hand away. "I'm not brave,' I said, continuing to back into the living room.

"Yes, you are." She jumped at me, poking me again. It really did hurt.

I tried to move away but my leg connected with the corner of the coffee table, tripping me. I reached out and grabbed Lucy, pulling her down with me. She squealed.

We landed on the carpet, me on my back, Lucy on top of me.

She was breathing hard and laughing. "I win."

I looked into her blue eyes. "Do you really think I'm brave?"

She narrowed her eyes for a second, as if trying to decide if I was being serious or joking with her. When she decided I was being serious, she said, "Of course you're brave, Alex. You saved my life. I don't know anyone braver than you."

A moment passed between us and we moved our heads closer to kiss.

But before our lips touched, the smoke detector in the kitchen began wailing its high-pitched alarm.

"The breakfast!" I said.

We scrambled to our feet and Lucy ran to the stove, taking the smoking frying pan off the gas ring. I grabbed a hand towel and waved it beneath the smoke detector mounted in the ceiling near the door to the aft deck. "How bad is it?" I shouted above the alarm.

"Not too bad," Lucy said, flipping the hash browns with a spatula. "They'll just be well done."

I opened the door to let some fresh air inside and continued clearing the smoke with the towel until the alarm stopped. I went back to the stove and continued cooking breakfast while Lucy poured the coffee.

We stood in silence, me flipping the hash browns, which were very dark brown on one side, and pouring the canned tomatoes into a pan while Lucy watched me, taking a sip of her coffee every now and then.

After a few minutes, she said, "Alex, I'm scared."

"So am I." I turned off the gas and used the spatula to place the hash browns and sausages onto two plates on the counter. As I added the tomatoes, I looked at Lucy and said, "Sometimes I think that going back to Apocalypse Island is a stupid idea. We could just sail out to sea and live on the boat like we did before."

"Before you heard your brother on the radio," she said. "I know there's no way you can sail off into the sunset until you find him. You didn't abandon me and you wouldn't abandon him either. Or your parents."

She was right. If we sailed away now, I would always wonder what had become of Joe, and our parents. And I would always wonder if I could have saved them.

"Hey," I said to Lucy. "We might find your family while we're delivering the antivirus."

She shook her head and tears pooled in her eyes. "You heard your brother's voice. You have a glimmer of hope. I've already accepted that my family is dead. We know what it's like on the mainland. I just hope that they are actually dead and not…you know." The tears spilled onto her cheeks.

I put my arms around her and held her tight. She cried against my chest for a few moments and then pushed away, wiping her eyes with the back of her hand. "Come on, let's eat breakfast before it goes cold."

We took our plates to the dining table and ate quietly. Heavy drops of rain began to spatter against the windows and onto the deck.

As we finished eating, I heard a shout from outside. Stepping out into the rain, I crossed the foredeck to see Sam on the deck of the *Escape*. He was wearing his Savatage tour T-shirt and jeans and was grinning while he held out his hands to catch raindrops. "Hey, Alex, it's a great day to go into zombie territory," he shouted.

I nodded but didn't share his enthusiasm. There were no great days anymore; all the great days were behind us.

All I could see ahead of us were days of pain and sorrow.

CHAPTER 2

A N HOUR LATER, WE WERE heading back to Apocalypse Island, sailing through the pounding rain and rough waves. I sat in the pilot's chair on the bridge, peering through the water-streaked windows at the gray sea and sky as I followed the *Escape* across the waves toward the island.

Every now and then, I glanced at the coastline hidden in mist and drizzle. Somewhere on the mainland, Jax was loose and probably leaving a path of destruction in her wake. For all I knew, Vess, the other Type 1, had escaped the confines of Alpha Two and was also roaming the land.

I had blamed myself for Jax's escape from the boat but Lucy had made me see that, if not for being injected with the pure virus at Apocalypse Island, Jax would never have turned into the monster she was now. It was Hart's fault, not mine, that Jax was on the mainland wreaking havoc.

And now I was going to be working for the organization that ran Apocalypse Island. It didn't sit well with me.

All my life, I had distrusted and rebelled against authority of any kind. In my shitty job, before the apocalypse, I had hated the bosses simply because they controlled me. I had sold my soul for a crap wage and they knew I needed the job to pay the rent. So they could give me the mind-numbing tasks and I would accept them without a complaint. As far as they were concerned, they had me for life.

The zombie outbreak had changed all that. Most of the people I had worked with were probably now dead, or shuffling around with blue skin and yellow eyes searching for prey.

And I was alive.

But now I was going to work for yet another company and follow their orders. And I wasn't even getting paid.

And as far as shitty tasks went, traveling through a zombie-infested country to deliver an antivirus beat anything I had ever been asked to do in my old job.

I had to remember that I was doing this for myself, so I could find my family, and help the other survivors. I might be working for the scientists that had caused this mess, but I wasn't part of their organization. Once the job was done, I was taking Lucy and my family, if they were still alive, and sailing out of here. I wouldn't look back.

In the distance, beyond the *Escape*, the dark shape of the island appeared against the backdrop of gray sky.

My stomach roiled. It was all very well deciding to sail away after the job was done, but surviving that long wasn't going to be easy.

***

Apocalypse Island loomed over us as we moored our boats alongside the others at the dock. The rain was still coming down in full force, hissing off the island's rocky cliffs and the concrete blocks that formed the dock.

We were all dressed in waterproof jackets from the storeroom. They were dark blue with the 'Sail To Your Destiny' motto embroidered in small avocado-green letters over the right breast. They were fine for keeping the rain out but the waterproof fabric was noisy whenever we moved. The jackets were equipped with hoods but we didn't use them; we needed to be alert and aware of our surroundings. Apocalypse Island was just as infested with zombies as the mainland.

The four of us waited on the end of the dock. It was too dangerous to walk up the asphalt path that cut through the cliffs to the woods beyond. Sam and I had learned that lesson the last time we'd come here.

"How will they know we've arrived, man?" Sam asked.

"They'll see us on the cameras," Tanya said, indicating a camera bolted into the cliff face. The red light on top of the cylindrical steel body was glowing.

We stood close enough to the boats that if zombies or hybrids came down that path, we should be able to cast off before they reached us.

The rain bounced off the dock, the boats, and our waterproof jackets. Except for the splash of raindrops hitting the sea, there was no other sound.

"Maybe there's nobody here," Lucy said softly.

I knew what she was thinking. Maybe Site Alpha One had been overrun by zombies and hybrids. It was possible. The compound was protected by a fence and they had Hart's security team to protect them from the nasties, but his team wasn't that big and if an infected person got inside the perimeter fence, all hell could break loose.

Site Alpha Two had fallen, so why not Alpha One as well?

If that was the case, if there was nothing left on this island except a building full of zombies, all hope of distributing the antivirus was lost.

"This could be zombie island, man," Sam said, obviously following the same train of thought.

"We were here only three days ago," Tanya said. "There's no way the facility has fallen that quickly. Besides, they would have vaccinated themselves with the antivirus. They're like us; they can't be turned."

"But they can still be killed," I said. "Just like us."

13

She looked at me and nodded solemnly.

We stood in the cold, hissing rain for another five minutes before Lucy said, "I don't think anyone is coming to meet us."

"Agreed," Tanya said.

I sighed. They were right; Hart and his team should have been here by now. We were wasting our time standing on the dock in the pouring rain. We either had to go up to the facility on foot, or leave.

"What are we going to do?" I asked.

Lucy said, "If they haven't come down here, there must be a good reason. Either they can't come right now and will arrive later, or something has gone wrong and there's nobody left at the facility. If we go walking up there and something bad happens, we'll be trapped. I say we stay here."

I nodded. "I agree. We should stay with the boats. Maybe we should also leave the dock and sail out to deeper water."

"No arguments from me, man," Sam said.

"Me either." Tanya was already unhitching the rope that tethered the *Escape* to the dock.

I moved quickly and did the same for the *Easy*. Now that we had decided to leave the island, I wanted to do so as soon as possible. Something wasn't right here, and we weren't going to go blundering into whatever trouble had befallen Site Alpha One.

Climbing the ladder to the bridge, I shouted to Tanya, "Let's take the boats out half a mile."

She nodded and started up the *Escape's* engines.

I did the same and guided the boat away from the dock and into the choppy, deeper water. When we were half a mile out, I dropped the anchor and climbed down to the aft deck before going inside and taking off the waterproof jacket. I hung it on a brass hook near the door and ran my fingers through my rain-soaked hair.

Lucy was sitting by the window, watching the island through the rain-streaked glass. "What do you think has happened?"

I shrugged and sat down next to her. "Maybe nothing. It could be that they're just busy right now."

"Too busy to see us, the people who are going to deliver their antivirus for them?"

She had a point. The scientists at Site Alpha One were dedicated to the task of making the antivirus. That task was pointless unless there was a way to deliver the antivirus to the survivors on the mainland. Because Marilyn MacDonald, the director of Apocalypse Island, wouldn't let any of her own people do that job, it had fallen to us. We were an important part of their plan.

They wouldn't ignore our arrival unless there was a good reason to do so.

I grabbed a pair of binoculars and watched the dock where we had stood moments ago. The rainclouds passed over the island, scudding toward the mainland on the

15

breeze. The sun made a reappearance and shone on the dock, brightening everything with its warm light.

"Did you hear that?" Lucy asked. "It sounded like gunfire."

I shook my head. Then I heard it too, a distant cracking sound.

We went out onto the aft deck and listened. Out here, the sounds were clearer. They were definitely gunshots. I could hear single shots and the rat-a-tat-tat of automatic weapons.

And below that, the rumble of vehicle engines.

Sam and Tanya had emerged from the *Escape* and were standing on the deck, looking toward the island.

"What's happening, man?" Sam asked.

I shrugged, peering through the binoculars but unable to see anything because of the high cliffs.

The radio on the bridge crackled to life. "Alex, are you there?" It was Hart's voice.

I handed Lucy the binoculars and climbed the ladder to the bridge, picking up the mic and saying, "Hart? Is that you? Over."

"We're on our way to the dock," he said. "ETA two minutes. Over."

"We'll be there," I said. "Over."

"And, Alex," he added, "you'll need to get into the vehicles fast. We've got problems. Over and out."

CHAPTER 3

E MOORED THE BOATS AND grabbed our weapons before heading along the dock to the asphalt track. The sounds of vehicles and gunfire were louder now, closer to our position.

A Jeep came tearing down the track and skidded to a stop in front of us. Hart, sitting in the driver's seat, shouted, "Get in!"

We scrambled inside. I was riding shotgun, and the others were in the back seat.

Hart revved the engine and spun the vehicle around, accelerating up the track and crunching through the gears.

"What's happening?" I asked as we sped toward the trees. Up ahead, I could see three other Jeeps idling by the side of the track. Members of Hart's security team were standing by the vehicles, firing into the woods.

"Things are getting worse on the island," he said. "The zombies have been attacking the perimeter fence. Some of them got into the building. We cleared them out, but we've been fighting them ever since."

We raced past the other Jeeps and Hart picked up the radio mic. "Blue Team, return to base when ready." I heard shouts from behind us, then the other vehicles began following us back to the facility.

"This," Hart said, gesturing at the woods around us, "is the same problem we're going to have on the mainland. Even if we administer the antivirus to every single survivor so they can't be turned, we still have to deal with the zombies and hybrids that are already around. Sure, they won't add any more to their number by biting people and infecting them, but it's going to take a long time to eradicate them."

"The army should be able to wipe them out," I said. "Eventually."

Hart grimaced. "Sure, eventually. And in the meantime, those monsters will be killing every living person they come across. They won't be able to turn us, so they'll try to destroy us."

"The virus is adapting its tactics," Tanya said from the back seat.

"Yeah." Hart nodded grimly. "Everyone on the island has been vaccinated now. It's like the virus knows there's no point trying to spread itself to the population here so it's trying to kill us off instead. The same thing is going to happen on the mainland once we get the antivirus to the population there. It's going to be bloody war."

"As far as the virus is concerned, an unvaccinated person is a potential host," I said. "It wants to infect them so they can then infect others. But people who can't be infected are simply an enemy. So the virus will direct its hosts to kill them. It makes sense."

"Yeah," Hart said, "And then we have the hybrids that already want to kill everything. It's a shit storm."

The trees ended and the facility came into view. I could see places where the fence had been damaged. Bodies of zombies and humans littered the ground both inside and outside the fence.

"We don't even have time to clean up the dead bodies," Hart said as we passed through the gate and into the compound. His face was grim and I wondered how many of the dead he had known personally.

We parked by the main doors and got out of the Jeep. Hart swiped his access card through the digital lock and the glass doors slid open, allowing us into the foyer.

He led us to the elevator and we rode it up to level 3 where the lecture halls were located. Hart opened a double door and gestured us inside.

The lecture hall was the same one we had been in before, when we had been briefed about Site Alpha Two. Sam, Tanya and Lucy took seats in the front row. I sat in the row behind them. I had never been a front row type of person and didn't feel like starting now.

Besides, the last time we were in here, I had sat in the front row next to Johnny and Jax. Now, Johnny was dead and Jax was a monster. I wasn't sure if I believed in omens or not but I couldn't bring myself to sit next to Lucy, Sam, or Tanya just in case something bad happened to them. Stupid, I know, but I wasn't taking any chances.

Hart strode up the steps that led onto the stage and stood next to the large screen there. He looked toward the back of the hall and said, "Lights, please." The lights went down and the screen flickered to life, displaying two simple words:

OPERATION: WILDFIRE

CHAPTER 4

"OPERATION WILDFIRE," HART BEGAN, "HAS one main objective: to deliver the antivirus to as many survivors as possible on the mainland. The first phase of the operation will be to get the antivirus to military personnel."

"Screw that, man," Sam said.

"Yeah, screw that," I agreed. "It's the military that kept the first vaccine from the civilians. They don't get to keep this one all for themselves as well."

"It isn't that simple," said a female voice from the back of the hall. I turned to see Marilyn MacDonald walking down the aisle between the seats. She was dressed impeccably in a dark blue blouse and black trousers. Her blonde hair was piled neatly on top of her head, and her makeup was perfect. Looking at her, you wouldn't know that there was a zombie apocalypse happening right now.

21

She looked as if this was just another day at the office for her and not a last ditch attempt to save the country from zombies.

She stepped up onto the stage and addressed us. "When we sent the first vaccine, the faulty one, it was supposed to be distributed to everyone. The army took it upon themselves to vaccinate their own personnel."

"All the more reason to give this vaccine to the people," Tanya said.

MacDonald nodded. "In principle, I agree with you. But we have to think in practical terms. Every soldier has been vaccinated with the original, faulty, vaccine and that means they are all potential hybrids. Once a soldier has been vaccinated with the new antivirus, they can't be turned anymore. So by injecting them first, we destroy the chance of them becoming hybrids."

"And in the meantime, normal civilians can still be turned into zombies," Tanya said. "That's not right."

"I know it's not easy to hear in these terms," MacDonald said, "but slow zombies are easier to deal with than the hybrids."

Tanya shook her head. "So if a soldier becomes a hybrid that's a big deal but if an innocent civilian becomes a zombie, that's not so bad because they can be dealt with. Is that what you're saying?"

MacDonald put her hands on her hips. "As I said, it's not an easy choice but we have to perform this operation in a practical manner that will give the best chance of survival to everyone."

"By saving the soldiers," Tanya said, crossing her arms and sinking into her seat as if she were sulking.

"You know this makes the most sense," MacDonald said. "Once we take the potential hybrids out of the equation, we will commence with phase two of the operation and vaccinate the civilian survivors in the camps."

"If there are any left," Tanya muttered.

MacDonald had either not heard Tanya or had chosen to ignore her. She pointed a remote at the screen and the operation name disappeared to be replaced with a map of Scotland and the north of England. There was a red dot near the Scottish coast labeled 'Apollo' and a blue dot farther south and inland, in England, labeled 'Prometheus'.

MacDonald looked at Hart and said, "Ian, would you like to explain the details of the operation?"

He nodded and turned to us. "This marker here," he said, pointing to the red dot on the screen, "is the closest survivor camp to this island. Camp Apollo. It is also the only camp north of Camp Prometheus here." He pointed to the blue dot.

"The military has a transport infrastructure that crosses England and Wales, so if you can get the vaccine supplies to Camp Prometheus, they can do the rest, acting as a distribution hub for the army vehicles that travel those routes. That's how we distributed the original vaccine.

"Camp Apollo, however, is isolated up here in Scotland so they will need a separate delivery. And since that camp is much closer than Prometheus, it will be your first destination. There's a harbor close to the camp. It's part of a small fishing village called Muldoon. You can anchor there and unload the supplies for Camp Apollo."

Sam shifted in his seat. "How are we supposed to move the stuff from the harbor to the camp, man?"

"That's where your own ingenuity comes into play," MacDonald said. "This is why we need resourceful people such as yourselves to carry out this operation."

"I have a question," Lucy said. "Why don't you just use your helicopters to fly the vaccine to the camps?"

I grinned. Lucy and I had once had a conversation about *The Lord of the Rings* and I had told her that it would have been simpler if the eagles had simply flown the ring to Mount Doom so that it could be destroyed. I wondered if she was recalling that conversation now.

"We're grounded," Hart said. "The chinooks are virtually out of fuel and we have no way of getting more at the moment. The only way we can get to the mainland is by boat, the same as you. We will set up an operation to go get more fuel eventually but that isn't our priority at the moment."

I wondered if the lack of fuel was real or if it was just an excuse because MacDonald didn't want to risk her own people on this mission.

"So we're supposed to find a vehicle at the village and drive the supplies to the camp," I said. "At least Camp Apollo is near the coast. But Prometheus is inland. Are we supposed to drive all the way there too?"

Hart said, "You have a choice. You could drive south to Prometheus, or take your boats south along the coast and find a place to anchor. Then you'd need to find another vehicle to take you inland. It's about fifty miles from the coast to Camp Prometheus."

"How far is it if we drive from Camp Apollo?" Tanya asked.

Hart said, "From Camp Apollo, it's one hundred and seventy miles south to Prometheus."

"That's suicide," I said. "There's no way we'd be able to drive that far without coming up against hordes of zombies. There must be towns and cities all along that route."

"There are," MacDonald said.

"So we take the boats," I said. "It's a no-brainer. We anchor somewhere along the coast, find a vehicle, and drive the fifty miles inland to Prometheus."

"Plus the fifty miles to get back to the boats after we deliver the vaccine," Tanya reminded me.

I nodded. The first part of the mission, getting to Camp Apollo, didn't sound too bad. The only difficult part would be finding a vehicle to transport us and the vaccine to the camp. But the second part of the mission, a fifty-mile drive inland to Prometheus would be dangerous. And once we'd done the job, we would have to retrace our steps to get back to the safety of the water.

The operation wasn't what I had expected. I had thought that we would be delivering the antivirus to many different camps and that I could find Joe and my parents that way. If we were only going to two camps, how was I supposed to find my family?

"Each camp has a database that contains the name and location of every survivor in every camp," Hart said. "It's called the Survivor Board. When the camps started taking in survivors, they put their names and pictures on a board at the gates. I think it was to encourage other survivors to enter the camp, especially if their families or loved ones were inside.

"The information from the boards eventually became collated into a database and networked to each camp. Your brother's whereabouts will be on that database. The same goes for the rest of you; if your loved ones have survived and made it to a camp, you'll find out where they are from the Survivor Board."

We'd heard of the database before but our chances of getting into a camp to consult it had been non-existent. Now, we would be authorized to go into a camp, deliver the antivirus, check the Survivor Board, and leave without being shot.

I was sure that I was going to find Joe and my parents. Since the outbreak began, I had never been closer to finding them than I was now.

MacDonald turned off the screen. "We have maps, weapons, and supplies in the hangar. When you're ready, we can go down there and begin the operation."

There was no point hanging around here any longer. We got up from our seats and left the lecture hall, led by MacDonald and Hart.

We were ready to begin Operation Wildfire.

CHAPTER 5

THE HANGAR HOUSED THE THREE chinooks that Hart had said were out of fuel. There was also a truck loaded with cardboard boxes, its loading doors open. The place smelled of oil, gasoline, and rubber. There were mechanics tinkering with the engines of a couple of Jeeps and a crew doing something inside one of the choppers. The hangar was a busy place.

"Each box," MacDonald said, indicating the boxes in the rear of the truck, "contains a thousand pre-loaded syringes. Each syringe is in a white plastic tube printed with instructions for self-administering the intramuscular injection. The tubes protect the syringes, so they can take rough handling if the situation calls for it."

"How many boxes do we need to take to Camp Apollo?" I asked.

"Just one box. There are less than a thousand military personnel there."

"How many survivors?" Lucy asked.

"Around four thousand."

"So if we deliver five boxes," Lucy said, "that will vaccinate everyone in the camp."

"You will deliver one box to Camp Apollo," MacDonald said. "The others go to Prometheus for distribution among the armed forces. Once they are delivered, you will return here for more batches of vaccine. Those will also be delivered to Prometheus. Are we clear on that?"

"It's clear what you want us to do," Lucy said.

MacDonald looked at each of us, obviously gauging whether or not we would follow her instructions. She knew that once we were away from the island, we were on our own. We could do whatever we wished with the vaccine.

But what choice did she have? She wasn't willing to send her own people into danger, so we were her only hope of getting the vaccine to the mainland. If some of it went to the civilians and not the army, that was the price she was going to have to pay for our services.

She said, "Hart will give you the maps and supplies, as well as the identity cards that will ensure your safe passage in and out of the camps. Good luck." She turned on her heels and left the hangar.

"I think we pissed her off, man," Sam said, grinning.

Tanya gave Sam a high-five.

Hart sighed. "You really should consider running this operation the way Marilyn wants it to be run. Her reasons are sound."

"Well, it's not her going out there and risking her neck," Tanya said.

Hart nodded, resigned to the fact that there was nothing he could do to control us once we were out of here. Injecting us with the pure virus wasn't going to work again; we were all vaccinated. And we still remembered what had happened to Jax. We weren't going to let that happen again. This time, it was our way or the highway.

He led us to a long table that held weapons, maps, MRE packs and equipment. An Asian man in a white lab tech's coat sat at a laptop, waiting for us. Attached to the top of the laptop was a camera.

"You'll need to have your photos taken for your ID cards," Hart said. "If you have any trouble with military personnel, just show them the cards. Officially, you'll be working for us, which means you'll be working for the government."

We lined up in front of the laptop to have our photos taken. After that was done, the tech took the laptop and left the hangar, presumably to have our cards made.

"Speaking of the government," I said to Hart, "where are they? I assume they're still running the country, or what's left of it?"

He nodded. "They are. MacDonald is taking her orders directly from them."

"So they're here?" I asked.

"No, they aren't here. They're giving orders via video link. Their location is classified, of course."

"Of course," I said. They were probably safe in a bunker somewhere while the country they were supposed to be running went to hell.

"We have maps, weapons, and equipment over here," Hart said, changing the subject and walking along the table to the supplies. "There's also army clothing for you if you want it. You might find it more useful than your T-shirts and jeans."

He was right about that. The army trousers had more pockets than our jeans, and would dry quicker after getting wet. The combat jackets would be warm. There was even a selection of black army boots of varying sizes for us to choose from.

The maps had been marked with the locations of Camp Apollo and Camp Prometheus. They had also been weatherproofed with some kind of laminate spray. I picked one up and studied it. Apollo wasn't far from Apocalypse Island and it looked close enough to the coast that we shouldn't have too much trouble getting there. Although by now, I should know that nothing was simple. Not when there were zombies everywhere.

Camp Prometheus was located at a place called Killington Lake, about fifty miles south of the city of

Carlisle. I could see a route that we could drive from the coast to the camp, avoiding the city. That place was probably crawling with nasties.

"Do we know what state the roads are in?" I asked Hart.

He shrugged. "The army is keeping some of the main roads and motorways open but the smaller roads could be dangerous."

I nodded and folded the map before stuffing it into my pocket. I wasn't expecting this mission to be easy, but there were a lot of variables that were unknown. I didn't like the unknown; it usually meant trouble.

I moved along the table to the weapons. As well as the handguns, which I ignored because I still had my Desert Eagle on the boat, there were half a dozen M16 machine guns and a stack of magazines.

"We don't know how many zombies or hybrids there will be in the area," Hart said. "It will be best if you take plenty of firepower."

"Cool," Sam said, picking up one of the M16s and examining it.

I followed Hart along the table to a supply of flashlights, binoculars, Leatherman multi-purpose tools, hatchets, knives, lengths of paracord, stacks of MRE food packets, and protein bars.

"There's a lot of food here," I said. "This operation shouldn't take all that long."

Hart looked at me with a serious look in his eyes. "We all know what it's like out there, Alex. It's best to be prepared."

The tech guy came back into the hangar and handed us our ID cards. I looked at mine. It was laminated and had a photo of my face next to the words, "Harley, Alex". Beneath that was a string of numbers and a bar code. Beneath the bar code was the crest of the Ministry of Defense, a crowned wreath encircling crossed swords, a bird, and an anchor.

Welcome to government work. Come for the retirement plan, stay because you got zombified.

"Okay," Hart shouted to the mechanics in the hangar. "Let's get this stuff to the dock and onto the boats."

CHAPTER 6

I STOOD ON THE DOCK, watching while the truck was unloaded and the boxes were taken aboard the *Easy* and the *Escape*. Hart's team of men moved quickly and efficiently, taking the boxes, weapons, and equipment below decks while a second team crouched in firing positions on the asphalt path, weapons pointed back the way we had come.

A tense atmosphere hung over the area. We all expected a group of hybrids to come running out of the woods and down the path, teeth bared.

But that didn't happen. After a few minutes, the boxes were stowed and we were ready to leave. We had even been provided with Zodiacs so that we could keep the *Easy* and the *Escape* out in the deeper water while we went ashore.

The late morning sun had burned the earlier rain from the dock and boats, turning the day dry and warm.

If it wasn't for the fact that we were about to set sail for a zombie-infested mainland from a zombie-infested island, the day could almost be called pleasant.

"Good luck out there," Hart said as his men returned to their vehicles. "At least it's a nice day."

As he and his team drove the Jeeps and truck back along the path to Alpha One, Sam, Tanya, Lucy, and myself stood silently watching them. We were all thinking of the task that lay ahead of us. This day was not going to be "nice". Our mission was dangerous and possibly deadly, and from the moment we set foot on the mainland, everything would probably turn to shit.

"Let's get out of here, man," Sam said, breaking the silence that had descended over us.

I nodded and began untying the ropes that held *The Big Easy* to the dock. Once that was done, I jumped on board and climbed up to the bridge. It felt good to be sitting in the familiar pilot's chair again. The boat felt like home now, and it was the only place I felt safe.

All of my life, I had spent a lot of time in a place that was my sanctuary from the outside world. Growing up, it had been my bedroom. I had spent a lot of time in there, reading books and playing video games, much to my parents' chagrin. I'd had few friends but that was fine by me; I enjoyed my own company.

Later in life, it had been my house. I had locked myself in most weekends, playing games, reading books, and watching movies. Apart from a few outings with my friend Mike, I withdrew from society most of the time.

Now, my sanctuary was *The Big Easy* and the safety it provided. And my separation from society was not just the result of social anxiety; it was my best chance for survival.

Compared to my old life, though, I had more connections with the people around me now. Sam and Tanya were my friends. We had been through life-and-death situations together, and nothing connects people more strongly than a shared experience like that.

And, of course, I had a strong bond with Lucy. I couldn't imagine surviving without her. We had fought together side by side and witnessed the deaths of our friends. We had shared in each other's sorrow and grief. But as well as the dark moments, we had shared good times, and the bond between us had strengthened as a result.

I heard her coming up the ladder and I turned in my chair. Lucy climbed onto the bridge, dressed in combat boots, jacket and trousers. The jacket was open at the front, showing a white T-shirt beneath. She had pulled her long blonde hair back into a ponytail and she smelled faintly of the peach shower gel she used.

"How do I look?" she asked, doing a little turn so I could appreciate her from every angle.

"Like G.I. Joe's wet dream," I said.

She smiled and leaned against the wall, looking through the windscreen at the *Escape* sailing ahead of us. "I can't wait to see that database of survivors."

"Yeah, it should be interesting."

"I'm not expecting any of my family to be in there," she said. "I can't get my hopes up, only to have them destroyed."

"Even if they aren't on the database, it doesn't mean they aren't still alive," I said. "There are other survivors like us, staying away from the camps."

She nodded but her eyes were sad. "I know that. But my parents aren't the type of people who would be able to thrive in...all this shit. If they didn't make it to a camp, they won't be alive."

"I thought your dad taught you how to shoot."

"He did. But my mother is very ill. She can barely get out of bed most days. I know that Dad will try to protect her. He'd rather die with her than live without her."

"Maybe they're both okay," I said. I knew my words wouldn't give Lucy any hope; we both knew how bad the situation was. But I didn't know what else to say I wasn't even sure if my own parents were still alive.

I'd heard Joe's voice on the radio and knew that he and my parents had made it to a camp but that had been a long time ago. The way things were now, you could be alive one minute and dead the next. Or undead, which was probably even worse.

Lucy said, "We're going to tell the soldiers at the camp that the vaccine is for everybody, right?"

"That's my plan," I said. "We're out here risking our lives, so we should have a say in how this all plays out. The people in those camps have just as much right to be vaccinated as the soldiers. Fuck MacDonald and her rules."

She smiled and touched my shoulder lightly. "I'm glad we found each other again, Alex."

"Even though you went sailing away without me?" I joked, looking at her and raising a quizzical eyebrow.

She lifted her hand from my shoulder and brought it down again in a fist, her mock punch bringing a mock, "Ouch!" from me.

"It was you who went off half-cocked into the fog and left me!" she said.

"Okay, okay, I won't do anything half-cocked."

"Are you sure?"

"I'm sure," I said. "Especially while you're wearing that army gear."

She punched my arm again and went to the ladder. "I'll get the weapons and supplies ready to go. Are you going to be wearing army stuff when we go ashore?"

"I sure am."

She frowned.

"What's wrong with that?" I asked.

"Don't you hate it when couples wear the same thing?" She grinned at me and descended the ladder to the aft deck.

I turned back to the instrument panel, a huge grin on my face.

Even the rain pattering against the windows couldn't dampen my mood.

The warm glow I felt from Lucy's words only faded as we neared the rainy coastline and I saw a village and harbor in the distance. As we sailed closer, I could see rows of stone houses whose dark windows looked vacantly out over the sea. A couple of dozen fishing boats floated in the harbor, abandoned and neglected.

I pointed the binoculars at the houses and streets, looking for movement or any other signs of life.

The village called Muldoon looked as cold and dead as the grave.

The radio crackled, and Sam's voice cut through the static. "This is the place, man."

"Yeah," I said. The hairs on the back of my neck prickled as I looked at the silent houses and streets. I wanted to turn the boat around, head back out to sea and forget all about this dead village.

Instead, I dropped the anchor and climbed down the ladder to the aft deck. While *The Big Easy* rolled on the gentle waves, I surveyed the scene on the shoreline again.

I didn't believe that this place could be totally abandoned.

Lucy came out onto the deck. "Something wrong?"

"I'm just wondering where all the people are."

She looked at the village. "Maybe they all went to the camp."

"Maybe," I said. Then something caught my eye in one of the windows. I was sure I'd seen movement. I brought the binoculars up to my eyes and tried to find the window, my senses disoriented momentarily by the sudden magnification.

I found it and adjusted the focus on the binoculars.

As the image sharpened, I felt a chill along my spine.

Looking at me through the glass was an undead woman. She stood partly in shadow but her hateful yellow eyes were easy to see. They were locked on our boat.

Then another zombie appeared next to her. This one was a man. He was dressed in a dark blue sweater that was tattered and bloody. He stared out at us with the same malevolent expression on his face.

Movement in the house next door caught my attention. I swept the binoculars across to the windows there to find more zombies, all of them watching us with their yellow eyes.

"They're everywhere," Lucy said. Even without the binoculars she could see the zombies that were appearing in every window of every house.

"They must have heard us coming," I said.

"And they're all inside because of the rain." She looked up at the dark clouds. "If we'd arrived when it was sunny, they would have been out on the streets."

"Probably." I lowered the binoculars. "So what do we do now?"

"It's simple," she said. "We pray it doesn't stop raining before we find a vehicle and get out of here."

CHAPTER 7

WENT BELOW DECK AND changed quickly into combat boots, trousers, and jacket. When I got back up to the living area, Lucy was sitting at the dining room table. On the table, she had placed two M16s, the Desert Eagle, and a pair of small handguns. There were also stacks of magazines and an array of equipment. Boxes of the vaccine waited by the door.

I noticed that Lucy had put five boxes there, enough to vaccinate all of the soldiers and civilians at Camp Apollo.

"Do you think we're going to need all this stuff?" I asked, pointing to the guns and equipment.

"It's better to be prepared," she said. "When the rain stops, those zombies are going to come flooding out of the houses in search of prey."

"Let's make sure we're not here when that happens," I said.

She nodded and pushed one of the small handguns toward me. "You might want to take this instead of the Desert Eagle. It's a Walther PPK, and much easier to carry and handle than that cannon."

I picked up the small gun. It was lighter than the Eagle, that was for sure. And the name was familiar. "Walther PPK," I said. "The same gun James Bond uses."

Lucy nodded. "Now, let's get sorted. We'll take an M16 each and divide the magazines equally."

I put one booted foot on boxes of vaccine and posed with the Walther. "Harley. Alex Harley. License to kill zombies."

She groaned and said, "Technically, you can't kill zombies; they're already dead. Come on, put these magazines in the ammo pouches on your belt."

"I was just trying to lighten the mood," I said, detecting her annoyance at me. I couldn't blame her. We were both frightened and running on adrenaline. In my case, that made me try to make light of the situation. In Lucy's, it made her more serious.

I decided to keep my mouth shut.

We went out on deck and untied the Zodiac before lowering it into the water, loading the boxes and guns, and climbing aboard. Lucy started the engine and piloted us toward the *Escape*.

Sam and Tanya were waiting on the aft deck, dressed in military clothing and holding M16s.

When they had climbed down into the Zodiac and Lucy was taking us toward the harbor through the drizzling rain, I felt a familiar feeling of being out of my depth. I might be dressed like a soldier and armed to the teeth, but I had no military training. I was just an ex-gamer-turned-survivor.

Sam had worked with the survival expert Vigo Johnson and visited hostile environments all over the globe. Tanya had been a journalist in the Middle East and other war zones. Lucy had shooting experience and had spent her life staying fit.

And here I was, the odd one out. Dressed like a *Call of Duty* player at a cosplay convention.

Lucy tapped my shoulder. I turned around to face her.

"Everything okay?" she asked.

I nodded, then turned around again to face the front of the boat, watching the harbor loom larger as we approached. I had to squint to keep the rain out of my eyes. I wished I had brought my diving mask.

I couldn't tell Lucy what was bothering me. She would say I was being stupid and remind me that I had saved her life. That was true, and I had faced some overwhelming odds at Site Alpha Two.

Lucy would say that counted as experience, but I had the nagging feeling that I had only survived this long because of sheer luck. I didn't feel any more able to deal with the zombie apocalypse now than I did when we were in Wales with Mike and Elena and first heard about the outbreak.

"Those fuckers better stay in their houses," Sam said, his voice breaking me away from my thoughts. There seemed to be zombies at every window, watching us quietly. They weren't going crazy or clawing at the glass or moaning with hunger. I almost wished they had been, because their watchful silence was creepy.

The only sounds were the humming of the engine and the splash of the Zodiac cutting through the water.

Lucy guided it around the fishing boats to a small pebble beach and then killed the engine, allowing the front end of the Zodiac to scrape over the pebbles before we all climbed out. Sam took the mooring line and tied it to a metal stake that had been driven into the ground.

"Let's find a vehicle and get out of here," Tanya said.

"What about the boxes?" I asked, pointing the barrel of my M16 at the wet cardboard boxes in the Zodiac.

"We'll get a vehicle," she said, waving her thumb to indicate Sam and herself. "You two bring the boxes."

I nodded. That made sense.

The gray clouds were parting, showing clear blue sky beyond. The rain was barely more than a drizzle.

I didn't have to tell the others that we needed to hurry. Sam and Tanya jogged across the beach to the road that led from the harbor to the village. Lucy and I followed with the boxes, our army boots crunching over the pebbles.

"This is so creepy," Lucy said, watching the faces in the windows. "They look so calm, standing in their houses and looking out, but they can't wait to come out here and kill us."

"Let's hope they don't get the chance," I said, quickening my pace a little.

"They were normal people once," she half-whispered to herself. "Just like us. They probably loved living in this quiet village."

"I'm sure it was a nice place when there weren't zombies peeking through the curtains," I said.

We reached the road. It led up to the rows of stone houses and wound through the village. I couldn't see any vehicles parked outside the houses.

Sam and Tanya were standing by the village pub, which was named *The Kingfisher* according to the wooden sign above the door. They seemed to be waiting for us, so Lucy and I increased our pace until we reached them.

"Got a problem, man," Sam said as we set the boxes on the ground. They weren't heavy but their bulk was awkward and my arms ached a little from carrying them.

"What is it?" I asked, leaning the M16 against the pub's low wall and shaking my arms to get the blood circulating again.

He pointed along the street. The narrow road was littered with vehicles. Cars, vans, and trucks had been parked so that they blocked the road, the only way in or out of the village. And all of the vehicles had been disabled. Their tires were flat and it looked like their engines had been destroyed. Engine parts and wires lay scattered on the road.

Some of the cars had been burned out and were now only charred metallic shells. Others bore black scorch marks where flames had licked the paintwork.

"What the hell happened here?" I asked out loud.

Tanya answered, her eyes scanning the vehicles, which were now only so much scrap metal. "It looks like the villagers barricaded the road. They probably thought they could keep themselves safe from the madness that was going on in the rest of the world by keeping it out. It's like when the plague swept the country in the Middle Ages and townspeople and villagers kept strangers away in case they carried the disease."

"But why destroy all the cars?" Lucy asked.

I pondered that for a moment. I could see why they might barricade the road to keep strangers away but why wreck the vehicles as well? When the answer came to me, I felt a tinge of sadness for the people who had lived here, who were now existing as walking corpses in the place they had spent their lives.

"They weren't keeping people out," I said. "They were keeping themselves in. They must have known that a virus was spreading among them and they were quarantining the village. They destroyed the cars so that nobody could leave."

"That's so sad," Lucy said. "They knew they were all going to die, but they still wanted to stop the virus escaping to the rest of the world."

I looked around at the stone houses. "This place is very isolated. Maybe they didn't know that the rest of the world was infected. By the time they found out, they had probably already destroyed the cars, their only chance of escaping the village."

Sam sighed. "Great. So we have to find a car somewhere else. Their act of self-sacrifice has caused us a big problem, man."

"We also have another problem," Tanya said. "The rain has stopped."

CHAPTER 8

ANYA WAS RIGHT. WE HAD been so busy looking at the barricade that we hadn't noticed the sky brightening. I picked up the M16. "We need to get back to the Zodiac."

I could hear doors opening all around us and the zombies, quiet until now, began to emit low, hungry moans.

"Fuck," Sam said. The road that led back to the harbor was crawling with zombies.

The people of this community had sacrificed themselves to stop the spread of the virus beyond their village, but that self-sacrifice had been pointless. They were all zombies now, controlled by the virus they had been trying to isolate.

"We're going to have to shoot our way through," Lucy said, lifting her M16 and aiming at the crowd of bodies staggering along the road toward us.

Zombies came from every direction, shuffling out of the houses and heading for us with arms outstretched. There were so many of them, I didn't think we had enough ammo to kill them all.

Every front door had opened now, and the rotting monsters filled the streets.

Only the pub was quiet. Its doors remained closed, its windows dark.

"In here," I said, stepping back to the door of the pub and twisting the cold metal handle.

The door was locked.

The sharp crack of gunfire filled the air as Lucy and Sam sent bursts of bullets into the brains of the advancing horde. But instead of moving forward, they were backing up as they fired. The way ahead was blocked by a mass of stinking, staggering creatures. The stench of rotting flesh made me gag.

I ran to the pub window and rammed the butt of the M16 against the glass. It shattered loudly. I threw the boxes inside and then scrambled through after them, tiny shards of glass cutting my hands as I clambered over the windowsill.

The pub was gloomy and smelled of stale sweat and beer. I swept the barrel of the gun around the room, bracing myself for an attack from the shadows. None came.

Tanya and Lucy climbed in through the window. Outside, I could hear more shots above the incessant moaning. Sam vaulted into the pub and spun around, sending a hail of bullets out onto the street. The noise of the gun was louder in here, making my ears ring.

"We need to keep moving!" Sam said.

Grasping arms and clawing fingers reached into the pub through the glassless window. Blue rotting faces with yellow eyes and gnashing teeth glared at us as we backed away from the opening.

Lucy fired her M16 in three-round bursts, standing calmly as she dispatched the zombies at the window one by one. Their heads jerked back as the bullets penetrated their brains. Dark blood sprayed wildly.

As each zombie fell, another took its place. It wouldn't be long before they climbed in through the window and overpowered us. We only had a limited number of bullets.

I went in search of an exit and found a door that opened onto a dark flight of stairs leading up to the next floor. "This way," I shouted to the others. "Bring the boxes."

I ascended the stairs, keeping the M16 pointed in front of me. The others came through the door and closed it.

"This won't keep them out for long," Sam said, sliding home a small bolt that was no thicker than a pencil.

At the top of the stairs, an archway led to a kitchen and a small living room. The air smelled of old cigarettes but there was no telltale rotting-meat stench. The owners of the pub were probably out on the street with the other zombies.

A banging noise came from the bottom of the stairs. The monsters were pounding on the door, trying to break it down.

Sam took up a firing position at the top of the stairs. He might have a good chance of defending the stairs for a short time as the zombies stumbled into the confined space, but eventually they would get up here.

I ran to the back of the living space, looking for another way out. All I found was a small bathroom and bedroom.

Stepping into the bedroom, I was surprised to see that the bed was made perfectly, as if whoever had last slept there expected to return soon. There was a dressing table with makeup arranged neatly across its top, and two dark wooden nightstands and a matching armoire. A faint odor of rotting meat hung in the air, making me check under the bed.

I crossed to the large window on the back wall and looked down. There was a small paved yard below, hemmed in by a tall wooden fence. Beyond the fence panel at the far end of the yard, a grassy expanse of dead ground followed the top of a small cliff along the coastline.

Tanya came into the room. "Any way out?"

"Not unless we can get down there," I said, pointing out of the window.

She took a glance at the yard below and nodded. She opened the window. Fresh, salt-tanged air rushed into the room.

"It's too far to jump," I reminded her.

Without answering, she reached into the pocket of her combat jacket and took out a coiled length of paracord. Unrolling it quickly, she scanned the room. "We need an anchor point." She went to the armoire and tested its weight by pushing against it. Seemingly satisfied, she looped the cord around the front legs of the armoire. As Tanya began tying knots, I looked at the cord snaking across the carpet. It looked very thin. "Do you think that's going to hold us?"

"Yeah," she said, thinking I had meant the armoire and not the cord. "The wardrobe is made of a heavy wood, probably mahogany. And whatever's inside it is pretty heavy too. Don't worry, it'll hold."

I nodded, unsure.

Sam and Lucy appeared. "The door is starting to give way," Lucy said. "It won't be long now."

"We're going out the window," Tanya told them.

They both nodded, bringing the boxes into the bedroom and then throwing them out of the window one by one. MacDonald had said the syringes inside were protected by plastic tubes, so being thrown out of the window shouldn't damage them.

Tanya took the loose end of the cord to the window and threw it out. It wasn't long enough to reach the flagstones below so we would have to drop the last few feet, but that was better than jumping out of the window.

"I'll go last," I said.

Sam and Tanya looked at me with quizzical expressions, but Lucy knew why I had volunteered not to leave until everyone else was safe. She knew I was thinking of the lighthouse and Elena.

"Alex, it's not your fault she died," she said softly.

"I jumped before she did," I said. "If I had just waited…"

"Then you'd both be dead," she said.

"We don't have time for this," Tanya said, climbing up onto the windowsill and taking the cord in her hands. "I'll go first and make sure the yard stays zombie-free. Follow me down in whatever order you like." She leaned back out of the window and began abseiling down to the ground.

When she had dropped the last few feet and was standing in the yard, she called up, "Next."

Sam looked at Lucy and gestured to the cord. "Ladies first."

Lucy looked into my eyes and said, "You shouldn't blame yourself for what happened to Elena." But I think she knew that I would always carry some pang of guilt.

She went out through the window like a professional rock climber, not a trace of fear on her face as she leaned back and lowered herself to the yard below.

54

The banging on the door to the pub was now accompanied by the sound of splintering wood.

"You sure you want to go last, Alex?" Sam asked.

"Yes," I said. "Just hurry."

Slapping me on the shoulder, he nodded and took the cord. "See you on the other side, man." Then he was gone, climbing outside and dropping out of sight.

A few seconds later, he called, "Okay, Alex."

I picked up the cord, noticing for the first time that my hands were sweating.

I heard a loud bang but it sounded much closer than the door downstairs.

It came again, and this time I saw the armoire doors shudder, then burst open. I jumped back in surprise, my back colliding painfully with the wall.

When I saw what was coming out of the armoire, my mind kept repeating, *Holy fuck, holy fuck, holy fuck!*

The zombie was a child, a girl of maybe ten or twelve. She wore a long nightgown that had once been white but was now stained with blood and dirt. Her long hair was matted and oily, her yellow eyes wild. Her mouth and wrists were bound with strips of cloth that had probably also once been white but were now as dirty and bloody as her nightgown.

She reached out for me with her bound hands. Her voice was silenced by the gag but her wild eyes telegraphed her intentions. She glared at me with such malevolence that she might be a demon right out of a horror movie.

The shock of her sudden appearance put me off my guard. I swung the M16 at her but by the time the barrel was pointing in her direction, she swatted it away with her arms and jumped forward at me.

I dropped the gun and used my hands to keep her away. With her mouth bound, she couldn't bite me, but her mouth worked beneath the cloth, instinctively seeking my flesh.

Her stench made me gag as I tried to hold her at bay. I wondered how long she had been festering in the armoire, rotting slowly among the clothes and shoes.

She lashed at me with her hands. As I fought her, I heard the door downstairs break open. Heavy footsteps sounded on the stairs, along with low moans as the zombies staggered up to this level.

Outside, beyond the window, Sam called, "Alex, you coming down, man?"

They didn't even know that I was fighting a zombie in here.

I pushed the girl away with as much strength as I could. She fell to the floor, leaving a dirty stain on the carpet as she struggled to get back up.

Grabbing the Walther PPK from its holster, I thumbed the safety off and shot the girl in the head. Blood and brains sprayed from the back of her skull and over the dressing table. Her body collapsed to the carpet and lay there.

"Alex!" Lucy called, panic rising in her voice.

I went to the window and clambered up onto the sill, breathing heavily. The first of the villagers crashed through the bedroom door. They barged into the room, snarling and gnashing their teeth.

I had no time to be worried about the distance to the yard below. I slung the M16 over my shoulder, slid across the windowsill, and tried to grip the paracord tightly enough to stop my descent.

I realized too late that my technique was all wrong. Instead of leaning back, letting the cord take my weight, and walking down the wall, I was hanging helplessly, my feet dangling in mid-air.

Through the window above me, I heard the zombies crossing the carpet, their stench adding to the already-foul air.

I wasn't going to be able to hold on much longer. My hands weren't strong enough to support my entire body weight. I felt myself slipping, the cord burning into the palms of my hands.

Three zombies, a man and two women, appeared at the window, reaching down for me with their rotting hands.

One of the women caught my wrist and tried to pull me up. I fought her, holding onto the rope with all the strength I had left and kicking my feel wildly to make myself more difficult to hold on to. That made me swing from side to side, the rough stone wall scraping against my arms and legs. I managed to get the soles of my boots against the wall, giving me leverage to pull against the zombie's grip.

I heard a shot from below and then the woman's rotting head jerked back in a spray of black blood. She released my wrist suddenly. Because I had been pulling against her, the sudden lack of resistance sent me swinging backward before I crashed into the wall again. All the air in my lungs exploded out of me as my chest hit the hard stone.

"Alex, drop down, man."

I looked down to see Sam standing there, arms outstretched as if he were going to catch me. He must have seen that I didn't have the strength to hold on to the cord any longer. Tanya was crouched in the firing position, her M16 braced against her shoulder. I assumed she was the one who had shot the zombie so accurately.

"I've got you," Sam said with a confidence that made me believe he could actually catch my weight and stay upright, like a father catching his daughter as she dropped lightly into his arms from a jungle gym at the playground.

I let go of the cord and went hurtling down toward him. Sam caught me in his arms, but my weight sent us both crashing to the flagstones. I lay on the cool stone for a moment, still winded and trying to catch my breath.

Sam staggered to his feet, looking as groggy as a drunk who had just fallen into the gutter and was trying to regain his feet. "Jesus, Alex," he said. "You need to stop eating all those steak dinners, man."

That made us all laugh. Our diet mainly consisted of canned food and frozen meat when we could get it, but none of us was eating heartily. I had lost a lot of weight recently but obviously not enough to make myself light enough to be caught from a high window.

"Hey, I'm big-boned," I said.

That made us all laugh again. At the window, more zombies had appeared, reaching for us and moaning despite the fact they couldn't reach us.

"Let's get out of here before they figure out how to get around here," Tanya said, picking up a couple of boxes and moving to the rear fence.

There was a trampoline in the yard. I wondered if it had belonged to the girl I had shot upstairs, the girl who had been shut away in the armoire.

"You should have dropped onto that," Sam said. "You'd go bouncing over the fence in no time."

"What happened up there?" Lucy asked me as she picked up a box of syringes.

"I'll tell you later," I said, lifting the other two boxes "When we're safe." As far as I was concerned, we might be out of the house but we were still in danger. We were the only humans in a village full of zombies. I wouldn't feel safe until we were back in the boats.

The fence panels around the yard were made of flimsy wood slotted into stone uprights. Sam put his shoulder against a panel and pushed against it. The wood broke out of the slot and fell to the ground. We stepped over it and onto the grassy clifftop beyond.

I looked for a route we could take that would lead us back to the Zodiac but the cliff face was almost vertical and the beach below was full of jagged rocks. My experience of trying to abseil out of a bedroom window and failing left me in no doubt that I wouldn't be able to get down this cliff without killing myself.

"This way," Tanya said, leading us along the clifftop. I glanced back at the village every now and then. We weren't being followed.

"What happened back there, Alex?" Lucy asked me.

"Yeah, man, we thought you'd decided to stay up there and play with the zombies," Sam added.

I told them about the girl in the armoire and how she had been gagged and bound.

"Her parents probably put her in there after she turned," I said. "If nobody else went into the room, she might have gone into that dormant state that takes over the zombies when there's no external stimulus."

"And we woke her up," Tanya said.

"Yeah." I looked back toward the house. That girl had been someone's daughter and they had been forced to shut her away, probably because they hadn't wanted to kill her. I wondered if her mouth and hands were bound because her parents had continued to live with her after she had turned and were making sure they couldn't be bitten.

And then, I guessed, they themselves had turned and the girl had been forgotten.

"She's better off now," Tanya said. "Better dead than…whatever the hell the zombies are."

I nodded. Breathing in a lungful of fresh sea air, I scanned the cliff for a way down. If we could get down to the beach below, we could double back to the Zodiac.

But Tanya veered away from the cliff edge toward a narrow road that led from the village and disappeared into the distance.

"Aren't we going back to the boat?" I asked.

She shook her head. "We need to find a vehicle to get us to Camp Apollo, remember?"

"I just thought that…since we couldn't get a vehicle at the village…we were going to go back to the Zodiac and search the coastline for a car or something."

"Waste of time," she said. "We're here now, so we might as well keep going. Retracing our steps will only slow us down."

I didn't reply. Being out here on foot, without a vehicle or a safe place to hide, made me feel exposed and vulnerable. There was nowhere to run if the shit hit the fan.

We reached the road. It looked barely wide enough for a single car and was pitted with potholes. Walking along the road was easier than trudging through the grass but my arms were aching from holding the boxes.

"There's a farm ahead," Lucy said, pointing to a wooden sign by the side of the road that said FRESH EGGS, NEXT LEFT. Above the words was a drawing of a chicken.

We increased our pace. I had no idea how far ahead the next left turn might be but the sign had given me a glimmer of hope.

It was fifteen minutes later when we found the farm. A narrow track led from the road to a stone house in the distance. Behind the house was a collection of barns and animal pens. As we walked along the track, I could hear chickens clucking from somewhere close by.

When I saw a dark blue Land Rover Defender parked by the side of the house, my heart leaped and I felt a sudden rush of optimism.

All we had to do was drive that Land Rover to Camp Apollo, deliver the boxes, and get back to the boats.

Maybe this mission was going to go according to plan after all.

CHAPTER 9

THE DAY HAD BECOME SUNNY and warm, and the Land Rover seemed to gleam in the sunlight. The smell of farm animals filled the air, along with the clucking of chickens. The birds were running loose in a field behind the house, along with a dozen cows that were lazily grazing on the grass there.

Sam went to the front door and tried it. After discovering that it was locked, he knocked on the wood. "Hello? Anyone home?"

I was sure that if I lived here and four people dressed in army clothing and carrying weapons strolled up the path and knocked on the door, I wouldn't answer.

Sam shrugged when there was no reply and went around the back. I put down the boxes I'd carried all the way from the village and rubbed my aching arms. Lucy did the same, going over to inspect the Land Rover after dumping her box. She used her hand to shield her eyes from the sun and peered in through the driver's window.

Tanya set down her boxes and sat on the front step, closing her eyes and turning her face to the sun.

I didn't know how she could be so calm because, despite my earlier optimism, I felt nervous now that we were at the house.

I heard bolts being drawn back and latched unlocked, then the front door opened and Sam stood there grinning. "Back door was open," he said.

"You get the Land Rover keys?" Tanya asked him.

He dangled them from his fingers.

"There's nobody in the house?" I asked.

Sam shook his head. "The radio is on but there's nobody home."

Now that he mentioned the radio, I could hear music playing faintly somewhere within the house. I went inside. The place looked like it hadn't been decorated in a long time and some of the cream-colored wallpaper that covered the walls was stained, with some of it damp and peeling in places.

The kitchen was large, with an old stone fireplace that had been bricked up at some point to create space for a large oven. The radio was on the kitchen counter, playing "Heaven is a Place on Earth" by Belinda Carlisle. The back door was open, revealing a small graveled area beyond, and the fields beyond that.

There were deep depressions in the gravel where a car had once been. Maybe the Land Rover had been parked back here at some point.

The air in the house smelled damp but there was no rotten-meat stench.

"Alex, are you coming?" Lucy called from the front door.

"Yeah," I said. I wasn't even sure why I had entered the house. I was curious to know what had happened to the owners but there was nothing here to indicate their fate. Belinda Carlisle faded out and Nick Tucker, the new Survivor Radio DJ, announced that the next song was dedicated to all the survivors left in the world. The Doors began to sing "Strange Days".

"Alex?" Lucy called again.

"I'm coming," I said.

As I passed the stairs on my way back to the front door, something upstairs caught my eye. I went up the first couple of steps to take a closer look, still wary even though I was sure the house was empty.

One of the upstairs doors was open and through it I could see a bedroom that looked as if it had been hit by a cyclone. The closet doors were open and there were clothes scattered over the bed and floor.

I went up to the top of the stairs and saw that the bathroom was in a similar state. The medicine cabinet on the wall was open and looked like somebody had rifled through its contents in a hurry. A smashed bottle of cough medicine lay in the sink, its dark brown contents congealed around the drain.

A noise behind me made me whirl round, gun raised.

It was Sam, standing halfway up the stairs. "Hey, man, we're ready to go."

"Okay," I said, following him down the stairs and out of the front door. The boxes were loaded into the back of the Land Rover. Tanya sat in the front passenger seat while Lucy sat in the back.

I climbed in the back next to Lucy and stowed the M16 by my feet.

"What was so interesting in there?" she asked.

"It looks like the owners ran away," I said. "I think there were clothes missing, and some of the medicines from the bathroom cabinet had gone too."

"The place was probably robbed," she said. "The back door was open."

"I don't think thieves would have taken the toothbrushes. There was an empty holder on the sink. Whoever lived there left in a hurry."

She looked through the side window at the house. "I wonder where they went."

Sam started the engine and revved it a couple of times before putting the Land Rover into gear and taking us along the path toward the narrow potholed road.

"They probably went to the harbor and took a boat," I said to Lucy.

"I don't blame them; they were living next to a village full of zombies." She sat back in her seat and looked out at the sea as we hit the road and bounced over the potholes.

I felt more relaxed now that we were in a vehicle. At least the Land Rover offered some protection if we were attacked.

Tanya unfolded her map and opened it on her lap. When the road we were on intersected with a wider, two-lane road, she told Sam to turn left. The wider road was much smoother.

In the distance, I could see a group of zombies shambling across a field together. I wondered if they were wandering aimlessly or if they were following a noise or movement that had attracted their attention.

We drove for almost an hour in silence, each of us lost in our own thoughts. I wondered how long it would be before I saw Joe and my parents again. I tried to convince myself that they were still alive. Joe had always been tough. He was a natural survivor. He'd be okay and would make sure that our parents were too.

I was dragged from my thoughts when Sam put the radio on. Nick Tucker was talking to a guest, which was something I had never heard on Survivor Radio before.

"So what is your advice to survivors, General?" Tucker asked.

A voice that was deep and confident replied, "Our advice to survivors is the same as it has always been. Find a survivors camp in your area and go there. Let us take care of you. It is too dangerous to try and survive on your own. If you don't know where your loved ones are, they are probably in a camp. We can reunite you."

Sam shook his head. "If you don't know where your loved ones are, they're probably dead, man." He reached to turn off the radio but I stopped him.

"Wait. I want to hear what he has to say."

"Why, man?" Sam said. "You know they just talk bullshit."

Tucker thanked his guest and then said, "Remember, people, you need to be in one of our camps if you're going to make it. There are signs on the roads and near every town and city denoting the location of the nearest camp. Go there now. I beg of you." He paused for dramatic effect, and then added, "Here is David Bowie and 'Life on Mars'."

"You hear that?" Sam asked. "They've got that DJ wrapped around their finger. 'Come to the camps, I beg of you'. He even said 'our camps'. I bet he's working for the military."

"We're working for the military," I reminded him.

"Well, it's not the same thing. We're not telling people lies."

"I don't think they're lying just because they've set up camps to help people."

"Those camps are there to control people," he said. "They've told everyone that the rest of the world is infected and it isn't true. People without hope are easier to control."

According to Sam and Tanya, the virus hadn't reached America. "Have you ever thought that they might be right? We don't know what's happened to the rest of the world. For all we know, the virus has spread across the globe. A lot of the survivors are safer in the camps than wandering around out here with the zombies."

He looked at me in the rear-view mirror. "Wow, you've changed your tune, man. I thought you hated authority. You've seen the camps. Do you really think anyone is better off in one of those makeshift prisons? Because I sure don't."

"I have to believe the camps give people a chance of survival," I said, "because my brother and parents are in one."

"Okay, man," he said, backing down slightly. "We'll have to agree to disagree. I hope your folks are okay."

"And what about the people who lived in that farmhouse back there?" I asked. "Do you hope they're okay too?"

He shrugged. "Of course, but what do they have to do with…"

"They were listening to the radio when they decided to leave their house and take their chances," I said. "They didn't even bother to switch it off when they left. What if they heard that broadcast you did and decided to bug out? They might have been safe enough in that isolated farmhouse but they heard that message and went for a boat to get to Europe. The nearest place they'd go would be Muldoon. There's a harbor there after all, and plenty of boats. They might have wandered into a village full of zombies because of you and your damned message."

Tanya turned in her seat to face me. "Alex, there's nothing wrong with telling people the truth. How they deal with it is up to them."

I ignored her and looked out of the window again at the fields rolling by. I wasn't really mad at her or Sam for doing what they thought was right but I hoped that their radio broadcast hadn't spurred Joe and my parents into leaving whichever camp they were in. If they were still in a camp, I could find them. If they were wandering in the wilds, we probably had zero chance of being reunited.

Tanya turned to face front again and gave Sam some instructions, pointing at the map as she did so.

We reached an intersection where the normal road sign had been covered over by a bright red sign with black lettering that read SURVIVORS CAMP. Next to the lettering was the same Ministry of Defense crest that was on our ID badges.

"Well, there's no chance of missing the camp," Tanya said, folding the map and putting it into her pocket.

Sam took the road indicated by the bright sign. High trees on both sides of the road blocked the view and most of the sunlight so that we were plunged into shadow. Knowing that the camp was close made me feel nervous.

Since the apocalypse had begun, I had spent most of my time running from the military or avoiding them. The thought of having to come into close contact with soldiers made me anxious.

My anxiety grew when, after we had driven for another twenty minutes, I saw a large red sign affixed to a tree. Like the other sign, this one bore the MoD crest and the words SURVIVORS CAMP, along with a thick black arrow pointing at a side road that led through the woods.

Sam slowed down and turned onto the smaller road. It was not much more than a dirt track, but I could see wide tire tracks left by other vehicles. The route looked like it was used frequently and had been used recently.

We had gone about a mile when Sam began to slow down. Ahead of us was a checkpoint, which consisted of a sentry box with a small gate that could be raised or lowered. At the moment, it was lowered and a sign on its metal grille said STOP.

The sentry box seemed to be empty.

Sam hit the brakes and put the Land Rover into neutral. "We need to lift the gate, man."

"I'll do it," I said. The area seemed to be deserted and I supposed that the soldiers who should be working the checkpoint were taking a break somewhere nearby. I opened my door and got out. Maybe I should call out. It could be that the soldier who should be manning the sentry box was taking a piss behind one of the trees.

I listened but the only sound was the low, idling rumble of the Land Rover's engine. I approached the sentry box, looking in through the window. There was nothing in there except an office chair, a table upon which an Andy McNab paperback lay face down and open, a small TV that was turned off, and the controls for the gate.

I tried the door. It was unlocked. I went inside and inspected the control panel. There was a green button marked OPEN and a red button marked CLOSE. It couldn't be any simpler. I hit the green button and the gate slowly began to rise up with a mechanical whirring sound.

I went back outside and got back into the Land Rover.

Sam waited until the gate was all the way up and then drove forward. As we drove farther along the path, I looked out of the rear window at the empty sentry box.

"Something wrong?" Lucy asked.

"Just wondering where the guards are."

"Me too," she admitted.

The trees gave way suddenly and the track crossed rolling grassland. Ahead of us was the camp. I saw a wire fence that must have been at least twenty feet tall and sentry towers that reminded me of the World War II prisoner of war camps you see in movies. Within the fences was a cluster of olive green tents of varying sizes from big marquees to one-person camping tents, and wooden huts that, again, reminded me of POW camps.

There was a main gate, above which a stenciled wooden sign said CAMP APOLLO.

The gate was open.

There were no guards in the towers and I couldn't see any movement within the camp.

"Nobody home, man," Sam said, bringing the Land Rover to a halt just outside the main gate and killing the engine.

"There should be five thousand people here," Tanya said. "Where did they all go?"

I kept my mouth shut. Tanya and Sam had broadcast a message on the radio telling people to leave the camps and now they were surprised that this camp was empty. Not wanting to return to the earlier argument, I grabbed my M16, opened the Land Rover door, and said, "Let's go take a look."

There might still be a computer here that was linked to the survivor database. I could still find out where my family was.

As I stood on the grass, which was still wet from the earlier rain, I felt a sense of unease. I couldn't put my finger on anything specific that was making me feel that way but I stood watching and listening, ready to scramble back into the Land Rover if something came rushing out of the trees or from the tents.

The others must have felt it too because as they exited the vehicle, they stood silently surveying the area before moving toward the camp gate.

I could hear the sound of my own rapid breathing, but nothing else. Camp Apollo was as quiet as a grave.

"Does anyone else feel like we're about to walk into a trap?" Tanya asked.

"Yeah, man," Sam said. He had turned to face the woods, his back to the camp, his eyes searching the shadows beneath the trees.

"Maybe two of us should stay out here," Tanya suggested.

"No way," I said. "We shouldn't split up." I'd seen more than enough horror movies to know that splitting up was never a good idea.

"Okay, then let's go," she said, moving forward warily.

We fell in behind her, weapons pointing in all directions as we made our way to the open gate.

A sudden sound made us all jump and I almost squeezed the trigger of my M16 before I realized that it as just a crow cawing somewhere in the woods.

Great. That was just what we needed right now, a creepy sound effect.

We reached the gate and paused. It was made of the same steel as the fences and was just as tall. A heavy steel bolt had been pulled aside, allowing the gate to be opened.

"It's intact," I said. "The gate was opened normally. It's not like something broke in."

"Or broke out," Lucy added.

I nodded.

"Maybe they closed down the operation here and moved somewhere else," Tanya suggested. Her voice was low and tight and I realized that we were all talking in hushed tones, as if someone might be listening to our conversation.

We proceeded through the gate and into the camp, passing between the unmanned sentry towers.

"I don't think they went anywhere," I whispered. "They wouldn't leave all these vehicles behind." I nodded toward an area near the gate where an assortment of military vehicles had been parked.

Most of the vehicles were in desert colors, with a few in woodland camouflage. There were Land Rovers, Jeeps, personnel carriers, and a large six-wheeled truck that had a cage welded around its body.

"Mastiff," Sam said. "I saw some of those in the Middle East. The cages can stop a mortar shell."

"They wouldn't leave equipment like that behind," I said. "Either everyone who was here is now dead or they had to depart quickly and abandon everything."

"Why would they do that?" Lucy asked. "It doesn't make sense. If they had to leave quickly, the vehicles would be the fastest way to travel."

"So that brings us back to everyone being dead," Tanya said, looking around at the tents and huts.

"Maybe we should leave," Sam said.

He had a point. Whether the people from Camp Apollo had run away or been killed, one thing was clear: this place was dangerous. But inside one of these huts could be a computer that would tell me where Joe and my parents were. I couldn't just walk away when I was so close.

"We should take a look around first," I said. "We might discover what happened here, and we might even find the Survivor Board database."

Sam shrugged. "Sure thing, man. It shouldn't take us more than a week to search the camp. There are more tents here than at the Glastonbury Festival."

"The tents are probably where the civilians lived," I said. "The wooden huts are likely to be the soldiers' quarters and offices. We should focus on those."

He looked at Tanya. I had noticed that in matters of importance, Sam always deferred to Tanya's judgment.

She nodded. "Sure, why not? We can take a look in some of the huts."

I led the way to the nearest hut, a long, low building with frosted glass windows and a single door. The others fell in behind me, obviously deciding that since this was my idea, I could go first.

I went up to the door and tried the handle. It turned in my hand and the latch clicked open. "It's unlocked," I said. I hesitated, wondering if I was going to push the door open and come face to face with a hut full of hybrids. Maybe they had been waiting in here quietly, willing us to open the door and release them.

Swallowing, I pushed the door and stepped back. The door swung open, slammed into the wall, and juddered. I hadn't realized that I'd pushed it so hard. My actions were being controlled by adrenaline.

The air that came rushing out to greet me was so fetid that I felt like I had been physically pushed backward by its foul stench. I retched, leaning against the side of the hut for support.

Sam peeked through the doorway, one arm held over his nose and mouth.

He stepped away from the hut, shook his head as if to try and clear it of the memory of what he had seen in there, and said, "That's some fucked up shit, man."

CHAPTER 10

SAM USED THE BUTT OF his rifle to break the frosted glass windows all along the length of the hut, letting fresh air inside to replace the stagnant putrescence that had come wafting out of the open door.

After a couple of minutes, my stomach had stopped twisting into knots and we tentatively entered the hut.

It was a morgue. Stainless steel tables stood in two rows that reached from one end of the hut to the other, forming an aisle in the center. The walls were covered with diagrams and charts, put up in a seemingly haphazard manner. Some of the diagrams were crudely drawn, others more professionally. All showed various parts of the human body.

On each stainless steel table lay a corpse. Some were zombies, others hybrids, and a couple looked human. All of the corpses were in various states of dissection.

Built into a corner of the hut was a Plexiglas box that reached from floor to ceiling. There was nobody inside it at the moment but I wondered who or what it had been built to contain.

The nearest body to us was that of a zombie. Its ribcage had been opened and was held by surgical clamps, revealing the creature's insides. Some of those insides had been removed. Its intestines lay on the table next to the body, along with its heart.

The creature's stomach lay on a separate, smaller table, cut open by a precise incision. The stomach's contents had either been taken away or long since dried up. The zombie's eyes had been scooped out of its head and placed in a jar of liquid that sat next to the stomach.

"What the fuck, man?" Sam asked nobody in particular.

"They've been experimenting on the zombies," Tanya said, walking along the center aisle while she inspected each corpse in turn. "I'm guessing these are people that turned while they were in the camp."

"And what about these two?" I asked, pointing to the two men who looked fully human. "They haven't been zombified at all. Why are they in here?"

"I have no idea." She inspected the human corpses. "It looks like they were shot. They both have gunshot wounds to the chest."

"Same as the hybrids," I said, looking over the three bodies that had the telltale roadmap of dark veins that denoted a hybrid. "Were the humans bitten?"

"Yeah," Tanya said.

"Maybe they were killed before they could turn," I suggested.

"Yeah," she said. "It's a bit more disturbing than that. Take a look at this."

I went over to the human corpses. They had been cut open and sewn shut again. Their bodies bore Y-shaped autopsy scars that ran from their shoulders to their groins. Tanya pointed at their wrists.

Each man had been bitten in exactly the same place, the right wrist, and the bite mark was at almost exactly the same angle in both cases.

"That didn't happen naturally," I said.

Tanya looked at me. "It's so precise, I'd say it was part of an experiment."

"But who would volunteer to be bitten by a zombie?"

She raised an eyebrow. "Who said they volunteered?"

I felt suddenly cold. "This place is run by the government. Do you think they sanctioned this?"

"Hell, yeah."

I needed some air. Despite the broken windows and open door, there was still a strong stench of death in here. I went outside and gratefully breathed in the fresh air.

I could understand the government wanting to dissect the zombies to see what made them tick. The same with dead hybrids. But those two men in the hut looked like they had been subjected to bites in the name of whatever weird science was being practiced here. They had been murdered.

Tanya appeared next to me. "You still want to go exploring more huts?"

"Maybe we can find a computer," I said. "It might tell us what happened here."

"Even if we found a computer, those files would be buried so deep, we'd never be able to access them."

I looked around at the city of tents and huts. "Something doesn't make sense, Tanya. Where is everyone? If they left, why did they leave the vehicles behind? These vehicles are worth millions.. They wouldn't just walk out of here and leave all that."

Sam was running his hand along the flank of the six-wheeled Mastiff. The sand-colored vehicle was huge, at least ten feet high and twenty-five feet long, the tops of its wheels almost as high as Sam's waist. "We've got to get the keys to one of these, man," he said, grinning.

Lucy was standing next to the Mastiff, hands on hips, looking up at the gun mounted on the roof.

"I don't know where everyone is," Tanya said. "I don't know why they walked out of here instead of driving. But I do know that if we find a computer, it will be password-protected and encrypted. This camp is a bust. We need to get back to the boats and sail down to Camp Prometheus. Hopefully that place won't have gone all Roanoke on our ass like this one has."

"Okay," I said. "You're right. It's just that I want to know where Joe and my mother and father are so badly. I keep thinking I'm getting closer to finding out and then it's snatched away from me."

She put a hand on my shoulder. "We all want to know who is on that Survivor Board, Alex. And we'll get a chance to look at it. But not here. There's nothing here but death."

I nodded. Our time would be better spent at the next camp, where there might actually be people, than in this abandoned place.

Looking over toward the vehicles, I saw Sam and Lucy opening a small hut and peering inside.

"Hey, we're leaving," I shouted.

Sam hesitated at the doorway. He shouted, "Be there in a minute, man," and then disappeared inside the hut.

Lucy came over to me. "He wants to drive that," she said, pointing at the Mastiff. The vehicle keys are in that hut."

I rolled my eyes. "We haven't got time to go joyriding." Now that we were going back to the boats, I wanted to get there as soon as possible. This camp gave me the creeps.

Sam reappeared with a set of keys in his hand and a grin on his face like a child on Christmas morning.

"We're going back to the Land Rover," I told him. "Meet us there when you're finished playing." I turned around, intending to return to the Land Rover, but when I saw Tanya, I froze.

She had already walked part of the way toward the open gate. But something had stopped her in her tracks. She looked like she had walked into a nest of rattlesnakes and was trying not to make any sudden movements. I followed her gaze toward the gate.

When I saw what was there, I muttered, "Oh, fuck."

Beyond the fence, coming out of the woods, was a horde of hybrids. There were hundreds of them, all dressed in military uniforms and walking out from the tree line onto the grassy area where we had parked the Land Rover.

Some of them had already reached the vehicle and were looking inside for prey.

"Sam," Tanya said, "how quickly can you get that thing started?"

"I'm on it, man." He opened the rear doors of the Mastiff and then went to the driver's door and got inside.

I remembered how many military personnel had been at this camp and I was sure there were a thousand hybrids just beyond the gate. A thousand pairs of yellow eyes gazed at us with murderous intent. Then the infected creatures came running through the gate and into the camp.

"Go!" Tanya shouted, turning on her heels and sprinting for the Mastiff.

I ran for my life.

CHAPTER 11

A S I RAN FOR THE Mastiff, I could hear the hybrids behind me. Their boots sounded like beating war drums. They were close enough that I could hear their breathing. And they were getting closer. I knew how fast the damned things ran and I wasn't sure I could get to the vehicle before they grabbed me.

Tanya and Lucy were already at the truck. But instead of jumping inside through the thick metal rear doors, they unslung their M16s and began firing at the hybrids.

The bullets screamed through the air close to my head. I resisted the instinct to drop to the ground. *Keep running. Just keep running.*

When I finally reached the Mastiff, the girls scrambled inside to give me room to get through the rear hatch. I jumped inside but as I did so, I felt something tug on my boot. I landed on the metallic floor of the Mastiff with a loud *ufff* as all the air blasted from my lungs. Before I had a chance to recover, I was being dragged back outside by a hybrid.

She had my boot gripped tightly in her hands and she slid me across the floor to the hatch. I kicked at her face with my other boot but she didn't even seem to notice.

Lucy screamed and grabbed my arms, trying to pull me back into the vehicle. I wasn't sure what Tanya was doing because my attention was focused on kicking the hybrid that had me in her grip.

Then a single shot rang out in the enclosed space and a hole appeared in the hybrid woman's forehead. She released me and fell to the ground.

"Sam, go!" Tanya screamed.

More hybrids appeared at the hatch, hands grabbing and clawing as they tried to force their way inside.

I scrambled farther into the vehicle and pulled out the Walther.

The engine roared to life and we lurched forward.

But we were going too slowly. The hybrids surged forward and one of them got inside. I kicked him hard and he staggered back before Tanya put a bullet in his head.

The Mastiff began to pick up speed but the hybrids were still matching our pace.

"We need to close the doors," I said.

Tanya began to shoot wildly into the mass of faces that appeared at the hatch. Lucy joined her, firing her M16 in three-round bursts.

I fired the Walther until it was empty. The air inside the vehicle smelled of cordite and my ears were ringing.

At last, we seemed to be moving fast enough to outrun the hybrids. I lunged forward for the doors and pulled them closed, locking them with shaking hands.

"Hold on," Sam said from the driver's seat, "we're going through the gate."

Metal screeched against metal as we hit the gate and went through it. Then I could hear the heavy thump of hybrids bouncing off the Mastiff's grille as Sam plowed through them.

I was breathing hard, trying to tell myself that it was all over, that we were safe for now.

"Everyone okay back there?" Sam asked as we drove onto the track that led through the trees.

"Yeah," Tanya said. "We're okay."

"There's gonna be a slight bump," Sam said. "Hold on." We rammed through the gate at the checkpoint. He turned to us, grinning. "This thing is pretty neat, huh?"

I sat up and looked around the interior of the Mastiff.

There were five fold-up seats attached to one side wall, and three on the other. They each had a four-point harness like those used by fighter pilots. The floor was made of bare, ridged steel, the ceiling covered in sand-colored fabric that housed the interior lights. A circular hatch in the ceiling led to what I assumed was the top-mounted gun. Below the hatch was an adjustable platform for the gunner to stand on.

An opening at the front led to the cockpit where Sam sat. There was an empty passenger seat next to him and an array of computer screens. Instead of being a single pane of glass, the windscreen was split into two side-by-side panes. Through them, I could see the trees and the track ahead. We were rumbling along at a decent speed.

Sam was right; the Mastiff was pretty cool.

"Who wants to sit up front?" he asked. He really was like a kid with a new toy.

I looked from Lucy to Tanya. I didn't mind sitting back here and I didn't want the earlier argument with Sam to be rekindled if we sat together on the front seats.

"You go ahead," Tanya told me. She must have assumed that I wanted to go up there because, after all, I was the gamer geek who played at being a soldier online.

"Yeah, you go and sit with Sam," Lucy said. "We'll stay back here and have some girl talk."

"Oh?" I asked. "What are you going to do, compare lipstick colors?"

"No," she said, "we're going to discuss the best way to kill hybrids."

I wasn't sure if she was joking or serious. I looked at Tanya, who looked as solemn as Lucy, giving me nothing to work with.

So I went up front and slid into the seat next to Sam.

"How awesome is this?" he asked. "We can drive this thing at night with the lights off. There are six cameras mounted outside, including night vision." He leaned across and turned on a screen in front of me. The display showed the track ahead.

"SDU," Sam said. "Situation Display Unit."

"We won't be driving at night," I reminded him. "We're going back to the boats. You'll have to leave the Mastiff at the village."

He looked a little disappointed. "I know that, man. I'm just saying what we could do if we had to."

"Well, let's hope we don't have to," I said. "This is great but I prefer the safety of the sea."

He shrugged and reached down to switch the radio on. When the sound of Duran Duran's "Ordinary World" came out of the speaker, I was grateful that the station wasn't broadcasting another interview. The last thing we needed was another rant from Sam.

Instead, he sang along with Simon Le Bon. Sam's singing voice wasn't great but I'd take it over an argument any day.

We got to the main road and Sam turned the Mastiff in the direction of Muldoon. "Hold on," he shouted back to the girls. "We've more of the creepy bastards coming this way."

I looked through the narrow windscreen. Ahead of us, a horde of hybrids was gathered on the road. Some of them came running straight at the Mastiff while others waited.

The first few runners had nearly reached us.

Sam increased our speed. "Get ready to die, fuckers."

But instead of letting the bulky Mastiff run them over, the hybrids leaped up onto the vehicle. I realized then that the grille that protected us also had a downside; it provided hand-holds and made it easy for the hybrids to swarm over the vehicle.

Two of them scaled the front grille and crouched in the hood, pummeling the windscreen with their hands. Their fists made a hollow thumping with each blow and left smears of blood on the glass.

"They won't break through there," Sam said.

I could hear more of them on the roof, pounding on the metal, trying to get in.

Sam used the Situation Display Unit to see where we were going, since the view through the windscreen was blocked by the hybrids trying to break the glass.

On the screen, I could see the main horde waiting for us. We reached them and although some of them jumped onto the Mastiff, others were rammed by the front grille. Their bodies thudded against the metal.

"Fuckers," Sam muttered.

His earlier bravado seemed to have waned slightly now that we had infected passengers on the outside of the vehicle. I wondered how many were actually hanging on to the grilles as we plowed through the main mass of camouflage-clad monsters.

"They can't get in here," Sam said in a low voice as the pounding in the vehicle's body increased in intensity. I was sure he was right but we had to shake the hybrids somehow.

"They're following us," Tanya said. She was looking at a second SDU screen set up in the back. I assumed she had switched it to the rear camera view.

"What are we going to do when we get to the village?" I asked nobody in particular. "We can't just stop the vehicle and get out."

"We'll figure something out," Sam said. The lack of confidence in his tone didn't reassure me.

"Sounds like a plan," I said sarcastically.

"If you have a better one, let's hear it, man."

I fell silent. I didn't have a better plan. And I wasn't trying to intentionally rile Sam. I was still feeling frustrated at our lack of progress in Camp Apollo, particularly the fact that I was no wiser about the location of Joe than I had been before we'd driven to the camp.

The only thing we'd achieved so far on this mission was to piss off thousands of hybrids.

"We can try to outrun the ones that are following us," Lucy said. "We should get to the village before them, which will give us time to get to the harbor and get on the Zodiac before they arrive.

"But the ones on the vehicle are coming with us no matter how fast we go. We've got to get rid of them if we're going to have a chance at the village. The zombies there will be enough for us to deal with. Throw in a half dozen hybrids and we'll never make it to the Zodiac at all."

Sam pointed at the two hybrids furiously pounding on the windscreen. "So how do we get rid of them, man?"

"We're going to have to go out there and shoot them off," Lucy said.

"Lucy, don't be crazy," I said. "This isn't *Mad Max*. If you climb out there, you could be killed."

She looked up at the ceiling where the hybrids were still trying to force their way inside. She looked scared but her blue eyes also held a flash of determination.

"Like Sam said," she told me, "if you have a better plan, let's hear it."

CHAPTER 12

LUCY AND TANYA BEGAN LOADING fresh magazines into their M16s. I did the same for the Walther that I'd emptied earlier. I wasn't happy with us risking our lives to get the hybrids off the Mastiff but, as both Sam and Lucy had pointed out to me, I didn't have any better ideas.

"Okay, how are we going to do this?" I asked the girls.

"There are three ways we can get outside," Tanya said. "The rear hatch, the top hatch, and your side door. Maybe you can open your door and lean out to take the two on the front of the truck."

"What about the ones on the roof? As soon as I open my door, won't they try to get me?"

"We'll deal with them," she said, stepping up onto the raised platform beneath the hatch in the ceiling. She had slung the M16 over her shoulder and was holding her Walther.

"We don't know how many are out there," I reminded her.

She looked at me with a determined expression on her face. "We will once I open this hatch."

I tried desperately to think up a better way to shake the hybrids from the vehicle but my mind was coming up blank. I'd read many books and seen countless movies where I had rolled my eyes at the dumb actions of the characters. In most cases, I could see a better way for them to solve their problem.

But having been in real situations like this, I knew that sometimes the brain gets locked into a certain way of thinking and blocks out other ideas. It restricts the options available so that the mind isn't overwhelmed into inactivity. Sometimes, you just have to act, and the survival instinct forces you into that action, even if another five minutes of thinking might have yielded a better plan of action.

My mind was now stuck on the idea of climbing out onto the exterior of the Mastiff and shooting the hybrids. It had locked onto that course of action as the best way to survive this situation and wouldn't let me think about anything else.

I placed my fingers carefully around the handle of my door and unfastened my harness.

"Maybe you should slow down while we do this," I told Sam.

He shook his head and gestured to the side mirror. "Can't do that, man. They're right behind us."

I looked at the mirror. The horde was no more than a quarter mile behind us.

"On three," Tanya said. "One, two…"

I wanted to tell her that I wasn't ready yet but I would only be stalling. There was nothing else to do now but open the door and pray I was a good enough shot to take out the two hybrids before I was thrown from the vehicle - in which case the horde behind us would kill me- or ripped apart by a hybrid on the roof.

"…three."

I pushed open the door. It was heavy, and the added wind resistance meant I had to put my shoulder behind the push. The door opened and I almost stumbled out onto the road. Bringing up the Walther, ignoring my hair blowing into my eyes, I squeezed the trigger. The hybrid closest to me staggered back, roaring in pain.

I hadn't killed him. He bared his teeth and lunged at me. I ducked back inside the cab, pulling the door closed. The hybrid almost went over the side but he managed to get a hand on the grille attached to the door. He snarled at me.

I wound down my window, pointed the gun at his head through the grille and fired.

He fell out of sight. In the side mirror, I could see his lifeless body lying in the grass by the side of the road.

In the rear of the Mastiff, Tanya had opened the roof hatch. The rattle of machine-gun fire filled the air.

The other hybrid continued to pound on the windscreen as if unaware that his companion was dead.

I opened the door again and took a shot at him. The bullet missed entirely because he simply turned to face me and came scuttling across the front of the Mastiff like a human spider.

Before I had the chance to retreat into the cab, a pair of strong hands grabbed my jacket and pulled me toward the roof.

For a moment, I was suspended over the road, the wind beating at me mercilessly. Then I was yanked up and slammed onto the roof. My Walther went clattering across the metal roof panels and out of sight. Luckily, the Mastiff was more than ten feet wide and had a raised metal foot-high wall around the entire roof, so I knew the gun wouldn't go over the edge.

Now on my back, I looked up to see a female hybrid with long blonde hair tied back into a ponytail looking down at me with evil yellow eyes. The move she had just used on me would have made any WWE wrestler proud.

I raised my legs and kicked her away, using the soles of my boots against her chest. She stumbled back but soon regained her composure and came at me, teeth gnashing.

I tried to roll to the side, aware that if I rolled too far, I would end up on the road and as good as dead. My move wasn't fast enough, though, and the hybrid landed on top of me, trying to bite my face. Her breath smelled meaty and I didn't dare wonder what her last meal had consisted of.

I used both hands to hold her at bay but she was strong and heavy and driven by a virus-fueled rage. It wouldn't be long before my strength failed and her teeth sank into my cheeks or neck.

Then a burst of M16 fire ripped into her and she fell on top of me, dead.

Pushing her away, I looked up to see Lucy crouched on the roof, M16 in her hands.

"Thanks," I said breathlessly.

She nodded and aimed her gun over the side of the vehicle to shoot at a hybrid that was hanging on to the side grille.

Tanya, who had also climbed up onto the roof through the top hatch, was at the rear of the Mastiff using the butt of her gun to knock another hybrid from the rear of the vehicle.

Before I had a chance to fully appreciate how well Lucy and Tanya were doing, my legs were grabbed from behind and I was pulled down over the windscreen and onto the hood of the Mastiff.

I had forgotten about the hybrid there.

The fall knocked the wind out of me as I landed painfully on my side. The sound of the engine was loud here and I could smell diesel fumes as I fought to suck air into my lungs.

The hybrid stood above me, looking down at his prey. Then he dropped toward me, snarling.

I rolled to the side. I knew I was at the edge of the hood but I had no choice. If I didn't move, I was dead.

My body rolled over the side of the Mastiff and the next thing I knew, I was hitting the road. My momentum rolled me forward and past the edge of the road into the grass. The world tumbled in my vision and I was aware of pain shooting across my shoulders and hips. I heard the engine of the Mastiff, which had been so loud in my ear a moment ago, recede as the vehicle continued along the road, leaving me behind.

CHAPTER 13

SCRAMBLED TO MY FEET, trying to ignore the pain I felt in every muscle. Ahead, the brake lights on the Mastiff shone red as Sam stopped the vehicle. He had seen me go overboard and was probably now watching me in the side mirror. He knew I was still alive and he wasn't going to leave me here.

I looked back along the road. If I didn't move fast, Sam wouldn't have a choice, he would have to drive on. The hybrid horde was gaining on us.

Lucy and Tanya appeared on the roof, waving at me to move my ass. The Mastiff began reversing toward me.

I tried to run as best I could but my hips seemed to have seized up. Gasping, I made my way toward the vehicle, hearing the approaching boots of the hybrids behind me as they ran along the road.

The girls disappeared from the roof and then the rear hatch opened. "Come on, Alex," Lucy shouted. I could hear panic in her voice, which made me wonder how close the horde was.

The lights glared red again as Sam applied the brakes. I reached the vehicle and Lucy and Tanya pulled me inside.

"Go, go, go!" Tanya shouted to Sam.

He hit the gas and the Mastiff lurched forward.

Through the open rear door, I could see the hybrids no more than twenty feet away.

Lucy closed the door. She was breathing heavily and her forehead was dotted with beads of sweat. "Are you okay, Alex?"

I nodded, unable to speak. Everything hurt, including my lungs and throat.

"I took out the guy on the hood for you," Tanya said.

After a few moments of heavy breathing, I asked, "How many of them were there?"

"Including the two on the hood, there were eight," Lucy said. "We shot five of them, knocked two onto the road by smashing their hands, and Tanya kicked one overboard."

"You weren't kidding," I said.

They both looked at me with questioning expressions.

I said, "You really were discussing new ways to kill hybrids."

They smiled and pulled down one of the seats, helping me to get into it and strapping me in with the harness.

"You okay back there, man?" Sam asked.

"Yeah, I'm good," I said. I was sure that nothing was broken. I was going to be bruised and sore for a few days, but I'd live.

Tanya went up front to sit with Sam. "Highway to Hell" by AC/DC was coming out of the speakers now.

Lucy buckled herself into the seat next to me and reached across to take my hand. "I was worried about you," she said.

I attempted a reassuring smile but I was sure it looked more like a grimace. "I fell off a moving truck. It was no big deal."

"No big deal," she said, laughing lightly. "Is this the same man who complained every step of the way up a mountain in Wales?"

I laughed. "Yeah, things change," I said.

Her face grew more serious. "I'm sorry you didn't get to look at the survivor database. Maybe at the next camp, you'll find out where your family is."

"Maybe," I said. After being disappointed at Camp Apollo, I wasn't going to get my hopes up anymore.

After a moment's silence, she said, "I can't wait to get back on the boat."

"Me too. It's the only place I feel safe."

She nodded and then said, "After this is all over, do you think we'll ever want to live on dry land again?"

"Probably not. I don't think I'd be able to relax in case there was another outbreak."

"Yeah, I know what you mean."

"Besides," I said, "do you think this will ever be over?"

Someday," she said. "We have the vaccine now."

"Sure, we have the vaccine but imagine how many hybrids there are out there. It doesn't matter how many survivors are vaccinated against zombie bites, there are thousands of hybrids waiting to kill them."

"The army will deal with them," Lucy said. "They'll find a way to wipe them out."

"Their resources are limited. Every hybrid means one less soldier. The military has lost so many personnel already. And how are they going to fight the hybrids? With tanks and infantry? They'll turn the country into a battle zone."

"It's already a battle zone," she said.

"Yeah," I said, looking toward the cockpit and out through the bloodied windscreen at the darkening sky. "I guess it is."

CHAPTER 14

T HE SKY HAD TURNED A dark, deep blue by the time we reached the potholed road that led to the village. I hoped that by the time it was fully dark, we would all be sitting in the dining area of the *Easy*, eating a warm meal and laughing off the day's events.

Then, after a good night's sleep, we could sail south tomorrow morning in search of a vehicle to take us to Camp Prometheus.

But first, we had to get to the Zodiac.

"What's the plan?" Sam asked from the driver's seat when we could see the village in the distance. "Whatever it is, we need to move quickly. Those hybrid bastards aren't far behind us, man."

"How about we drive through the barricade and all the way down to the harbor?" Tanya suggested. "Then we make a run for the Zodiac. Sam and I will lay down covering fire while you two get the boat into the water and get it started."

"You think the Mastiff will be able to get through those cars?" I asked Sam.

He patted the dashboard lovingly. "Hell yeah. Betty won't even break a sweat."

"Betty?" Tanya looked at Sam as if he had lost his mind.

"Big Betty, man. That's what I've named her."

He was taking his love for this vehicle way too far.

"Okay, let's do it," I said, checking that my harness was fastened tightly. I was hopeful that the Mastiff -I refused to think of the vehicle as "Betty"- could slam through the barricade. I just wanted to make sure that the impact didn't slam me into the opposite wall.

"Cool," Sam said.

I checked that all my weapons were fully loaded.

Lucy did the same. "This shouldn't be too difficult," she said. "All we have to do is run to the Zodiac."

I hoped she was right.

"Hold on tight," Sam said.

I braced myself. Lucy took my hand.

A sudden impact threw me forward against the harness. There was a screech of metal against metal. The Mastiff slowed down for a moment and then shot forward.

A second impact shook the vehicle.

Sam whooped and shouted, "We're through."

"Any sign of the zombies?" I asked.

"Oh yeah, they're everywhere."

Lucy tapped me on the shoulder and pointed to the SDU screen in the corner. The image showed the road ahead through the roof-mounted camera. The residents of Muldoon were on the road and coming out of the houses, shambling toward the Mastiff as it rolled through their village.

We drove past the *Kingfisher* pub and on toward the harbor. I could hear thumps on the front and side grilles as we collided with the zombies on the road.

"Nearly there," Tanya said. "Sam, park this thing as close to the Zodiac as possible."

"No problem, man."

The harbor seemed to be free of zombies. As long as we got the Zodiac in the water before the hybrids arrived, we should be able to get out of here without too much of a problem.

Sam hit the brake and killed the engine. Looking back at Lucy and me, he said, "Okay, let's do it."

I unbuckled myself and went to the rear hatch, which Lucy was already opening. We jumped down onto the pebbles and began to sprint across the beach to the Zodiac.

I glanced back the way we had come. The road leading up to the village was crowded with zombies. Sam and Tanya started to shoot into the mass of bodies. Some of the zombies fell.

When I turned my head to look in the direction I was running, I noticed that Lucy had reached the Zodiac but, instead of untying it from the metal stake, she was standing beside it with her head cocked to one side, as if trying to listen to something.

"Lucy, what's wrong?" I asked.

"Do you hear that?" She frowned, listening.

I couldn't hear anything above my heavy breathing. "Whatever it is, it doesn't matter. We need to get out of here."

Then Tanya shouted, "Get back to the vehicle!"

I halted, skidding on the pebbles. What the hell was going on? The zombies had reached the beach but there was no need to panic. We could get out of here if we...

Then I heard it too. A low buzzing sound.

"Run!" Sam shouted. He was already climbing back into the Mastiff.

Lucy started running back to the vehicle, abandoning the Zodiac.

I ran after her. "Lucy, what's happening?"

"I don't know. But it isn't safe out here."

We clambered back into the Mastiff. Sam had already started the engine and was reversing back up the road before we had a chance to close the rear door. I slammed it shut and turned to face the cockpit. "What the hell is happening?"

"Strap yourself in, man," Sam said. He sounded worried.

I got into my seat and fastened the harness. Lucy was buckled into the seat next to me again.

Zombies thudded against the rear of the vehicle as we reversed up the road and into the village.

"Why are we leaving the Zodiac?" I asked.

Then, the world beyond the windscreen became a flash of red fire. An explosion shook the Mastiff. Debris rained down onto the vehicle, pinging off the metal roof.

On the screen, I could see what was left of the harbor. Most of the boats were on fire. The beach had been torn up by the explosion. I couldn't see the Zodiac. There were zombie parts everywhere.

A second explosion rocked us. Sam kept his foot on the gas, taking us back through the village as fast as he dared. We rolled over debris as a line of houses collapsed.

The world around us had become a chaotic inferno of destruction.

"We have to get out of here," Sam said. "It's a drone. They're attacking the village with a drone."

CHAPTER 15

WHILE THE VILLAGE ERUPTED AROUND us, there was nothing I could do other than sit tight and trust in Sam's driving skills. We reversed past the pub. Sam twisted the wheel so that the Mastiff backed into a side street. Then he took the vehicle out of reverse and moved forward back onto the main street.

He floored the accelerator.

We shot forward toward the barricade of car bodies. Sam aimed for the gap he had already created when we'd entered the village and was accurate enough to guide the Mastiff through it without another collision.

Ahead of us on the road was the horde of hybrids.

A sudden explosion among their ranks sent bodies hurtling through the air. The road was ripped apart and black smoke spread across the remaining hybrids, the remnants of the road, and our vehicle.

107

The SDU screens showed nothing but blackness and the view through the windscreen was the same.

Sam turned the wheel sharply to the right. "We' re going off-road," he said.

We bumped along blindly until the smoke cleared and the screens showed us that we were driving over grassland.

"Where are the hybrids?" I asked. I didn't want any of the damned things jumping into the vehicle again.

Tanya adjusted the view on her screen. The hybrids were being bombarded with whatever missiles the drone was firing from the sky. Each time a flash of bright fire appeared among the horde, the ground beneath the Mastiff shook. "They've got problems of their own," Tanya said.

We continued driving away from the scene of carnage and destruction. When we reached the edge of the woods, Sam stopped the Mastiff and cut the engine.

Lucy looked at him. "We can't stop. What if it comes for us when it's done with the hybrids?"

"It won't," I said. "At least, it shouldn't if the drone operator is thinking logically. Those things are controlled by operators that can see the ground below the drone through a camera. They sit in a bunker somewhere and remotely control the drone to take out ground targets. It's like a video game.

"Whoever is controlling that drone has obviously been tasked with destroying zombies. They probably spotted the horde of a thousand hybrids on the road and followed them here. But they have no reason to attack vehicles. Zombies can't drive."

"Well, it sure seemed like they were attacking us at the harbor, man," Sam said.

I shrugged. "Maybe he didn't see us down there on the beach." But even as I said it, I doubted that had been the case. I'd seen drone operator footage on the internet and knew that the cameras on the unmanned aircraft showed a clear and detailed view of objects and people on the ground. When the drone had attacked the beach, the zombies had still been on the road. We had been the target of the attack.

"We should get out of here," Tanya said. "I don't trust that thing."

Sam started the engine and drove us over the grass and back onto the road. The road took us inland, past farmland and woods.

The drone didn't follow us.

"So how do we get back to the boats?" I asked.

Tanya unfolded the map and found our current position. "There's another village south of here. Maybe we can find a boat there and get back to the *Escape* and the *Easy*."

We agreed to try it. As we set off for the new destination, I felt my energy dwindle. I had hoped to be onboard the *Easy* by now, eating a hot meal and enjoying the feeling of safety I only had at sea. Being back on board seemed like a faraway dream now.

Night fell as we drove along the road to the next village. The sky turned an inky black dotted with shining stars. The moon was a bright silver orb. There was no light pollution here in this isolated part of the country, so the night sky looked clear and dramatic.

"You okay, Alex?" Lucy asked.

"Yeah, I just wish we were back on the boats," I said. "This was supposed to be the easy part of the mission and it's already turned to shit."

"We'll be back home in no time. We should make a nice dinner tonight. There are some steaks in the freezer."

"Sounds good," I said. But I wasn't optimistic about our chances of eating those steaks tonight. Nothing had gone to plan so far and I had a feeling that things were only going to get worse.

We drove in silence for half an hour, listening to Survivor Radio play a loop of eighties music. Then Sam slowed down and said, "Guys, I think this was the village." He killed the engine and we all stared out through the windscreen at what had probably once been a quaint fishing village on the coast.

Every building had been reduced to rubble.

"We should go and take a look," Tanya said. "There could be a boat in the harbor."

I agreed. If there was even a leaky rowboat, I was willing to take it as long as it meant we could get back to the *Easy* and the *Escape*.

Sam started the engine again and drove us slowly toward the ruins of the village. On the radio, Iron Maiden was playing "Run to the Hills".

Sam hit the brakes and pointed at the sky in front of us. The drone was difficult to see in the night sky. It was no more than a dark shape that blotted out the stars as it crossed in front of them.

"They're patrolling the area, man," Sam whispered, as if the drone could hear us.

We sat there for at least fifteen minutes with the engine idling, watching the drone as it flew back and forth along the coast.

"They haven't attacked us," Lucy whispered. "Maybe Alex was right and they only attack zombies."

"I didn't exactly say that." I wasn't going to take the blame if we became a target. "When that drone bombed the beach, there weren't any zombies there, just us."

Tanya turned in her seat to look at me. "Should we risk getting closer or not?"

When did I become the expert on drones? I shrugged. "I don't know."

"What other option do we have?" Lucy asked. "If we can't get back to the boats, what are we going to do?"

Tanya looked down at the map resting on her lap. "If we can't get to the coast because it's being patrolled, we only have one option: we'll have to drive to Camp Prometheus and get them to tell whoever is in charge of the drones that we need to get to our boats because we have the vaccine on board."

"Drive?" I said, shocked that she would even consider such a thing. "Hart said it's a hundred and seventy miles from here."

Tanya looked at me angrily, and I knew then that she was just as pissed off about us not being able to get back to the boats as I was. "What other choice do we have?"

I had to admit that I didn't have a better idea. But the thought of driving all that way, even in the Mastiff, filled me with dread.

"We'll check out the village before we go down that route," I said, silently praying that we would find some sort of craft that would take us out to our boats..

Tanya nodded. "Yes, we'll check it out. I don't want to drive to Prometheus any more than you do but it might be our only chance to eventually get back to the boats."

I hated the word eventually. I wanted to be back on board the *Easy* before dawn.

We set off at a crawl toward the ruins. All eyes were on the dark shape in the night sky, watching for any change in its flight pattern.

When we were within a quarter mile of the village, the drone banked steeply and headed our way.

"It's coming," I said, trying to stay calm.

Sam slammed the Mastiff into reverse and backed down the road, taking us farther inland.

The drone turned slightly and resumed its patrol pattern, ignoring us.

"We're not going to get close to the village," Tanya said. "They're not just hunting zombies; they're targeting anyone who goes near the coast, living or undead."

"I guess we know why," I said. "They're making sure nobody leaves. After the message you broadcasted on Survivor Radio, they probably think people might try to sail away."

"Alex, you're like a broken record." Sam was busy turning the Mastiff around on the road so that we faced inland but he wasn't so busy that he couldn't get mad at me.

"Well, excuse me for being pissed off," I said. "But it looks like your message to the people has ruined our chance of getting back to the boats. If you'd considered the results of your actions before taking over the radio station and getting on air, we might…"

"Hey, man, I seem to remember you being there at the time. You couldn't wait to get on the radio yourself."

"I was trying to find Lucy," I said. "I wasn't trying to start an uprising."

"I don't regret telling the people the truth, man."

"No, of course you don't. Only now, the army is patrolling the coast thanks to you telling the truth and we have to drive nearly two hundred miles across a zombie-infested wasteland."

"Stop arguing, boys," Tanya said. "Save your anger for the zombies. We're going to find somewhere safe to stop for the night. We've got a long journey ahead of us in the morning."

CHAPTER 16

WENTY MINUTES LATER, WE LEFT the road and drove across a field to the edge of the woods. Sam turned off the engine and said, "We need to check the area for zombies but this should be as good a place as any."

Lucy opened the rear hatch and climbed out. I followed her. The night was cool and dry with a slight breeze rustling through the trees. I stretched my muscles, trying to ignore the soreness I felt in my hips and shoulders. The fall from the Mastiff had left me with a few bruises, but I knew it could have been much worse.

Tanya came around the back of the vehicle with a handful of MRE packets. "I found these in the storage compartment earlier. You two check the area while Sam and I get a fire going."

"Sure thing," I said. Lucy and I checked our weapons before venturing into the moonlit woods. We listened for sounds that would give away the presence of zombies like footsteps in the undergrowth or a low moan but the night was quiet.

"It looks like the steaks are going to have to wait," I said as we walked deeper into the woods.

"They'll keep," she replied. Then she added, "Maybe you should go easy on Sam. He did what he thought was right at the time. He couldn't have known it was going to lead to this. Anyway, if they hadn't taken you to the radio station, we wouldn't have found each other again."

"I know," I said, "and I'm grateful to them for that. I'm not really mad at Sam. It's just this situation. We're setting off on a long journey tomorrow and that terrifies me."

"It terrifies me too," she admitted. "But it isn't Sam's fault. You said he hadn't considered the consequences of his actions but what about your actions toward him? He's not made of stone, you know. You're hurting his feelings when you blame him for everything that goes wrong."

"Not made of stone? Are we talking about the same person? Sam is so laid back he makes the Dalai Lama look tense."

"Sure, if you look at the face that Sam presents to the world. He's cool and calm and he calls everyone "man". But how well do you know the real Sam, the man underneath all that bravado?"

"Well, I don't," I admitted. "I always thought he was exactly the person he seemed to be."

"Alex, nobody is that shallow."

"I'm not saying he's shallow. He's just…Sam."

She stopped and looked around at the dark, quiet woods. "Come on, let's go back. There aren't any zombies out here."

As we walked back to the Mastiff, I said, "I didn't mean to hurt his feelings." She had made me feel bad. I hadn't known Sam long but I considered us to be friends. I'd taken my anger at the situation out on him and that made me feel pretty shitty.

When we arrived back at the Mastiff, Sam and Tanya had built a fire on a patch of bare ground near the trees. At the moment, only sticks and small branches were crackling and hissing in the flames. Larger logs were stacked nearby.

Sam was putting MRE food pouches into plastic packets and adding water from a canteen before folding over the tops of the packets and putting them into the MRE cardboard boxes. When he had done that four times, he set all four boxes against a fallen log, leaning them at a forty-five degree angle.

"Chicken noodles okay for everyone?" he asked when he saw us.

"What's with the water?" I asked, sitting down next to him. I hoped we could talk on a friendly level and repair any damage that may have been done to our friendship.

117

Also, I really didn't know what he was doing with the water and the pouches.

"Those are smokeless MRE heaters," he said. "You put the food pouch in with a heater pad. When water hits the pad, it makes it heat up. Some sort of chemical reaction. You close the whole thing up and put it into the MRE box until it heats up the food."

"Cool," I said.

"Hopefully not," he said. "I prefer my food warm."

"How much food do we have?" Lucy asked.

"Four more chicken noodles and eight meatballs in marinara sauce," Tanya said. "That's all there was in the Mastiff's storage compartment."

"We're gonna need to get some more food and water when we're on the road tomorrow," Sam said. "And some more fuel if we can get it."

Great. As if driving all that way wasn't dangerous enough, now we were going to have to stop somewhere and get supplies. We had a stockpile of MREs on the boats but, like idiots, we hadn't brought them with us on the so-called easy part of the operation.

Sam put a log onto the fire. It cracked and popped as the sap inside dried up in the heat. The wood-scented smoke drifted into the trees on the night breeze.

He passed the chicken noodle pouches around, along with metal forks that I assumed Tanya had found along with the food. I ripped open my pouch and put a forkful of the noodles into my mouth. These rations might not be the highest quality food in the world but at the moment they tasted as if they should be in a five-star restaurant. I had forgotten how really hungry I was until I tasted those noodles.

"These are amazing," Lucy said.

We all agreed. Then we ate in silence, enjoying the noodles. When we were all done, Lucy said, "Maybe we'll get to see the survivor database tomorrow."

"Maybe," Tanya said. She didn't sound too hopeful.

"Aren't there any names you want to look up on there?" Lucy asked her.

Tanya shook her head. "Not really. My parents retired to Hong Kong years ago. After I got a job that meant I had to travel all the time and my sister got married and moved to Colorado, they decided to go back to Kowloon where they both grew up."

"You have a sister?" Lucy asked, in a tone that said she wanted to know more.

"Yeah," Tanya said, looking into the fire. "Lisa. She's older than me. We haven't spoken in a long time. Years."

"If you don't mind me asking, why not?" Lucy asked.

"I don't know. We just lost touch, I guess. I was busy trying to get news stories all around the world and she was busy with her home life. She has a daughter now but I've never met her."

"That's sad," Lucy said. "I bet she'd like to meet her Aunt Tanya."

119

Tanya shrugged. "I just hope it isn't too late now. I lost touch with Lisa but there was never any real reason. I guess I just thought that there would always be time to contact her again. It would be easy to fly over to Colorado and see her family. But I never did it. Now, I don't know if I'll ever be able to."

"I'm sorry," Lucy said. "I didn't mean to pry."

"No worries." Tanya smiled at Lucy but I could tell that she was thinking about her family. A sadness seemed to settle over her. It was evident in her eyes and her slightly slumped shoulders.

"How about you, Sam?" Lucy asked, trying to change the subject but probably digging herself into a deeper hole. "Anyone you'll be looking up on the database?"

"No," he answered flatly. "My parents are in New York. So is one of my brothers. The other is stationed in the Middle East. He's a marine. I barely speak to my family."

"Oh, God, I'm sorry." Lucy looked into the fire and remained silent.

"Hey, no problem, man," Sam said. "My dad owned a software company and he was a company man through and through. He virtually lived at the office. Max, my brother, is following in his footsteps. I wasn't, much to my dad's disappointment.

"I wanted to see the world, and not just a piece of it through an office window, so I spent most of my time rock climbing, mountaineering, surfing, that kind of thing. I had no goal in life other than the next adrenaline rush."

"But you became a cameraman," I said.

He nodded. "Yeah, man. I was on an expedition to Everest a few years ago and I met Vigo Johnson. He'd just signed a contract with a TV network to make the Sole Survivor show. He needed a cameraman who could go to all the places he could and film him demonstrating survival techniques in the wilderness. I said I could do that, and he hired me. In between seasons, I did some freelance stuff in war zones.

"My parents flipped their shit when they found out I was living and working in the world's hot spots. Never mind that my older brother was doing exactly the same.

"They tried to convince me to change my life. I was in Pakistan when my dad rang me and said I needed to do what was right for the family and come home to take my place at the company. He said that it was too dangerous to do what I was doing and that I'd end up getting killed. I told him I was going to do things my way and he would just have to accept that. We've barely spoken since."

He threw another log on the fire and watched it blacken as the flames licked over it.

"What's your story?" Tanya asked Lucy.

"Well, my life was boring compared to yours," Lucy said. "I went to work on the weekdays and spent most of my weekends at home. My mother was very ill. Sometimes, I went hiking or camping on the weekends with my friend

Elena. She's dead now, but you probably know that. Alex and I were with Elena and her boyfriend, Mike, when the outbreak began. I'll look to see if my parents are on the survivor database but I really don't think they will be. My dad is the type of man who will never leave his wife, no matter the circumstances. And since she's bed-bound, I think that means they're both dead by now."

A tear rolled down her cheek. She wiped it away with her sleeve.

"That just leave you, Alex," Sam said. "We all know your story, man. Shitty job, no social life, video games and fast food."

I shrugged. Maybe he was trying to get me back for when I got mad at him earlier. But what he had said was totally true. And I wasn't ashamed of my life.

"The thing is," he added, "you've changed a lot since then. We've been through some shit and you've always held it together. I respect that, man."

"Thanks," I said. His words sounded heartfelt and I was truly touched by them.

"So what about your brother and parents?" he asked me. "Are they tough survivors like you?"

"I'd like to think so. Joe definitely is. He stuck up for me my whole life and he's always been strong, both mentally and physically. If he's looking after my parents, then I'm sure they're safe too."

"That's good, man."

"We should probably get some sleep," Tanya said. "We've got a long day ahead of us tomorrow."

We all agreed. And as Sam kicked dirt over the fire and the girls walked over to the Mastiff, I glanced toward the coast. Somewhere in the night sky, the drone patrolled the cliffs and beaches, cutting us off from the boats that had become our homes and sanctuaries.

Operation Wildfire had sounded simple when Hart had described it. All we had to do was deliver the vaccine. Now we were facing a perilous road trip through zombie territory.

Was any of this ever going to get any easier? I reminded myself that that was why we were delivering the vaccine in the first place, to try and put an end to this nightmare.

No matter what hardships we faced, if we could help save the country, it would all be worth it.

Sam slapped me on the shoulder and said, "What're you thinking, man?"

We walked to the Mastiff. I said, "I was just thinking that tomorrow is going to be a shitty day."

"You know it," he said as he went around to the driver's door.

I climbed into the back of the Mastiff and closed the rear hatch, shutting out the world.

CHAPTER 17

THE NEXT DAY, WE WERE on the road at six in the morning. A low mist hung over the fields and the gray clouds in the dull sky threatened rain. We were all tired. Sam and Tanya had slept in the front seats of the vehicle, leaving the rear compartment to Lucy and me.

We found a couple of sleeping bags rolled up beneath the front seats and laid them out on the floor, but it was uncomfortable lying on cold, hard steel. I barely slept, and when I did manage to doze, I had nightmares about Joe. In my dream, he had been turned and was lurching toward me with an angry look in his yellow eyes.

So now, as we drove south from Scotland to England, I was in a bad mood. Wherever we ended up tonight, I hoped there was a proper bed.

The others seemed just as tired as I was. None of us spoke as we drove along the road. The only sounds were the rumble of the engine and pop tunes being played back-to-back on Survivor Radio. I guessed that Nick Tucker was still in bed. The man had sense.

The road was deserted. I had thought that we might see other survivors but that wasn't the case here in Scotland. But then if any survivors saw the Mastiff rumbling along the road, they probably went into hiding. The army was rounding up everyone they could for the camps and they weren't taking no for an answer.

In a way, I could see why they had adopted a zero tolerance policy in getting everyone into the camps. This wasn't like any other evacuation where refusal to be rescued simply meant you might die. In the zombie apocalypse, if you weren't put into a camp, you were probably going to add to the number of zombies the army had to deal with later.

By seven, the sky was still dull but the rain hadn't yet begun to fall. Survivor Reach Out came on the radio. More tales of woe and lost loved ones. The desperation in the voices of the survivors looking for their sons and daughters, wives, husbands, and lovers did little to alleviate the depressed mood in the Mastiff.

But then, after the Reach Out segment had ended, a new DJ came on air. She sounded way chirpier than anyone had a right to be at this early hour. "Good morning, everyone. My name is Sasha Green and this is The Morning Show, a new radio program for all you survivors.

"Now, before we listen to some rockin' tunes, I have a public service announcement. We all know that zombies don't like the rain, right? Well, I've been asked to warn you not to try and fight the zombies with buckets of water. Apparently, some people have tried to do this and the outcome has not been good. So, zombies don't like rain, but they aren't afraid of a bucket of water, okay?

"Great, now to blow those morning cobwebs away, here's The Cars and 'Drive'."

I burst out laughing. The thought of someone trying to defend themselves against a horde of zombies with a bucket of water was too hilarious. I knew that people did dumb things but that had to be the dumbest I had ever heard.

Sam, Tanya, and Lucy were laughing too. The depressive atmosphere in the vehicle was lifted.

"Oh, man, can you imagine that?" Sam said. "Imagine their face when they threw a bucket of water on a zombie and it had no effect. What did they think was going to happen, that it would melt like the Wicked Witch of the West?"

That sent me into another spasm of laughter. When I was able to speak again, I said, "That person deserves a Darwin Award."

As if on cue, the rain began to fall. It pinged against the Mastiff slowly at first in sporadic bursts, then came down in a torrent. Sam flicked on the wipers. The road ahead became hazy as water bounced from its surface.

"Now this is what the zombies don't like," I said. "Hopefully we won't see many today if the weather stays like this."

Tanya, who had the map open on her lap, said, "Hopefully not, but the rain doesn't affect the hybrids, so we need to stay alert."

I was all too aware of that. The virus kept the zombies out of the rain and, I assumed, other extreme weather conditions, because the host bodies were rotting and it was trying to slow the process. But the hybrids were alive so the weather had no more effect on them than it had on any other living person.

I could hardly believe that some people had taken the zombies' avoidance of the rain to mean that they could be harmed by it. They took shelter purely out of a survival instinct, a need for the virus to keep the hosts functioning in the long term.

It was almost an hour later when Tanya said to Sam, "We should reach the motorway soon. There are motorway services a mile after that. You want to try to get fuel and food there?"

He nodded. "Sure thing. I bet most of the services will have been looted so we may have to try them all until we find one with fuel."

Sasha Green was reminding everyone not already in a camp to find one as soon as possible. Then she played Van Halen's "Jump".

Lucy said, "I wonder why they have new DJs."

127

"It's psychological, man," Sam said. "When they only had Johnny Drake or Nick Tucker, a lot of the air time was just music playing on a loop. One DJ can only do so much. If they get more DJs on the radio, they can persuade more people to go to the camps. It's the human touch.

"Survivor Radio has one purpose, to act as a propaganda machine for the government. So they get a pleasant female voice on here and more survivors will decide to go to the camps. The way the message is presented is as powerful as the message itself."

"Surely people aren't that gullible," I said.

"Hey, man, there are people out there attacking zombies with buckets of water."

He had a point. "Well, those people would be better off in a camp," I said. "They'd have more chance of survival."

Sam nodded slowly. "Yeah, you're probably right. I never thought of it that way□ ."

I decided not to say what came into my head, that he saw the world in black and white and that not everyone was an accomplished survivor like he was. Instead, I simply said, "I miss Johnny."

"Me too," Tanya said.

On the radio, Tiffany began to sing "I Think We're Alone Now".

Ahead of us, a blue sign said M74 SOUTH. Sam took the slip road and we found ourselves on the motorway.

Then all hell broke loose.

CHAPTER 18

THE SLIP ROAD LED US onto the motorway. The three lanes heading south were clear, with no cars in sight ahead of us, but across the median, past a low metal safety barrier that separated us from the three lanes going north, a group of cars was traveling on the motorway.

When they saw us, the occupants of the cars lowered their windows and began firing. The bullets hit the Mastiff's metal safety cage with loud clangs.

Because we were going south and the cars were going north, we passed them quickly. I heard their engines rev as they sped up, probably to get to the next junction so they could come off the northbound lanes, turn around, and follow us south.

"What the fuck?" Sam asked after the cars had disappeared. "Did anyone see how many of them there were?"

"I counted six cars," Lucy said.

"They'll be turning around and coming after us," I told him, although I was sure he knew that. He had already increased our speed.

Tanya put down the map and climbed out of her seat. She came into the rear compartment, stepped onto the platform, and opened the top hatch. "I'll show those fuckers who they're dealing with."

She stood so that the top half of her body went through the hatch. Then I heard whirring as the gun emplacement on the roof turned around to face rear.

Sam was grinning as he turned around to say, "They must be crazy if they think they can take on Big Betty."

Lucy turned on the Situation Display Unit to show the view from the rear camera. The motorway stretched out behind us and in the distance, coming through the rain, the six cars were throwing up sheets of water in their wake.

They had to be crazy to attack a military vehicle using civilian cars. Crazy or desperate.

The top gun roared and the road in front of the leading vehicle, a silver Mercedes, was cut up as Lucy adjusted her aim. Then a second round of shots sent the car spinning into the central safety barrier, black smoke trailing from its radiator grille.

Sam punched the air. "Woohoo!"

The other cars dropped back after seeing their leader crash into the barrier.

Then they all roared forward.

Two Volkswagen Golfs, one white, one black, took the left and center lane while a dark blue Astra stayed in the right-hand lane. Behind them, a silver Citroen Picasso and a black BMW hung back slightly. I could see men and women in the vehicles and it looked like they were dressed in civilian clothing.

A woman with dark hair hung out of the passenger-side window of the Astra, firing at us with a machine gun.

"Where did they get the weapons?" I wondered aloud as Tanya returned fire.

"They've probably attacked military vehicles before," Lucy said over the booming of the top gun.

The Astra exploded in a ball of orange flame. The Picasso swerved to avoid hitting the flaming carcass but over-corrected and skidded off the road, ramming through a fence and into a field.

The BMW accelerated to join the Golfs. Two men leaned out of the back windows, firing at us.

Tanya fired again and the shots tore into the white Golf. I saw the driver slump to one side, the windscreen in front of her face cracked open by a bullet. The car veered to the left and came to a dead stop.

That left the black Golf and the BMW. They were getting closer.

"I'm out of ammo," Tanya shouted down to us. "Pass me the M16."

I passed it up to her. Her legs disappeared through the hatch as she pulled herself up onto the roof.

131

"Maybe we should help," Lucy suggested, going to the rear door with her own rifle in her hand.

I grabbed my M16 and nodded.

She opened the door.

The noise of the vehicles cutting through the rain on the road filled the Mastiff, along with the roar of the engines and the cracks of the shots being fired from the BMW.

Lucy brought her M16 up and fired. The shots peppered the front of the BMW. The driver swerved slightly but remained on the road, accelerating toward us.

I heard shots from the roof. The front tire of the Golf blew and it slowed down but it kept coming until more shots from Tanya blew the windscreen apart and the car came slowed to a stop.

I fired my M16, trying to ignore the pain as the gun kicked against my sore shoulder. My three-round burst hit the BMW's bumper and right headlights.

Lucy and Tanya both fired at the same time and the entire front of the car seemed to erupt with gunshots. It peeled off the road and into the grass at the side of the road. The men hanging out of windows were shouting at us and firing but now they were too far behind us for that to matter.

Tanya climbed down into the Mastiff and closed the top hatch. Her hair and face were soaked but she was grinning. "Big Betty six, bandits zero."

Lucy closed the rear door and breathed a sigh of relief. I let out a sigh of relief myself but I couldn't' share in Lucy's jubilation. The people we had just killed were living, breathing human beings. They weren't infected with the virus, they weren't zombies or hybrids. They were people like us, trying to survive in the chaos that had overtaken everything.

I kept quiet about it. I knew that those people had been trying to kill us and it was an "us or them" situation. I knew that we had been justified in doing what we'd done. I just wished we hadn't had to do it in the first place, that humanity hadn't devolved into this state of savagery.

Tanya took her place next to Sam, shaking her wet hair to shower him with rainwater. He laughed and cried out, "I'm melting! I'm melting!"

That lightened my mood a little. I had to forget about the bandits back there on the road. They were, after all, bandits. They could have chosen to go to a camp or survive on their own without trying to kill other living humans but they had chosen to steal and kill to survive. I wasn't going to rejoice in their deaths but I refused to dwell on them.

By killing them, we'd probably saved the lives of many other people.

"Not far to the services," Sam said, pointing through the window at a sign that said SERVICES 1M. Beneath the words were the logos for McDonald's and Costa Coffee, and a symbol of a petrol pump.

"Anyone want a Big Mac?" Sam asked.

Nobody replied. We were all checking our weapons.

CHAPTER 19

WE LEFT THE MOTORWAY AND drove up the short road that led to the services, which consisted of a one-level building that housed the eating establishments and shops and a petrol station located near the exit road that led back to the motorway.

The car park outside the main building wasn't empty. There were twenty or so cars parked there. There were no people inside them.

Sam drove us into the car park and brought us to a stop near the glass doors that led into the building. The lights inside were off and all I could see beyond the doors was darkness.

"You guys want to check inside for food and water while Tanya and I get the fuel?" Sam asked, turning in his seat to face us.

I shook my head, looking at the dark building. "I don't think we should split up. It's too dangerous."

"I agree," Tanya said. "We'll all check out the main building and then we'll all go to get fuel."

Sam nodded. "Sure thing, man." He turned off the engine and said, "Let's go."

We got out of the Mastiff and stood looking at the doors, M16s in hand. "Let's make this quick," Tanya said.

I couldn't agree more. This place gave me the creeps.

We moved forward, Tanya in the lead, Sam slightly behind her. Lucy and I brought up the rear, checking behind us every few seconds.

When we got to the automatic doors, they remained closed. Either the power was out or they had been locked.

Sam smashed the glass with the butt of his gun and used his boots to remove the glass from one of the panels in the door.

We climbed through, one after the other. I went last, checking behind us before climbing through the broken door.

The dark interior of the building smelled of sweat and rotten food but I couldn't detect the telltale aroma of zombies. That didn't mean the place wasn't a bandit hideout, though.

"Let's find the shop and get out of here," Tanya whispered, turning on her flashlight. She sounded nervous.

We moved forward in a loose formation, Tanya and Sam taking the lead again while Lucy and I covered the area behind us. Our flashlight beams played off the walls and shop entrances.

We walked past the toilets and a dark, deserted Costa Coffee shop. The tables and chairs in the shop were arranged neatly as if the place was about to open to the public.

The next shop was a WH Smith bookstore that also sold food and drinks. There were no doors; the shop simply opened up onto the wide corridor we were walking along. We stepped into the aisles and searched the food shelves.

It looked like the place had been looted already. I found a couple of chocolate bars and Tanya found two plastic bottles of water that had rolled beneath a shelf. Other than that, the shop was empty except for the books and CDs.

"Damn it," Tanya said. "Let's get out of here."

A noise outside the shop, in the corridor, caught our attention. My heart began to trip along and I brought up the M16, pointing it at the darkness. "I don't see anything," I whispered. Our flashlights lit up the area directly outside the shop but there was nothing there.

I tried to recall the sound. It had sounded like a plastic coffee cup falling to the floor. So who or what had knocked it over?

"Let's head for the exit," Tanya whispered. "But slowly."

In formation again, we left the bookshop and stepped into the wide corridor. I saw movement in the coffee shop. It had looked like someone ducking behind the counter.

"There's someone there," I whispered, pointing my flashlight at the place I had seen the head duck out of sight.

Tanya hesitated and I knew what she was thinking. Should we check it out or leave here as fast as possible?

"Let's check it," she said.

We moved into the coffee shop quickly and I aimed my M16 and flashlight over the counter.

There were three people there: a man in his thirties, a woman of similar age, and a girl who looked like she might be nine or ten years old. They cowered against the counter.

"Please don't hurt us," the man said, his voice panicked. All three of them had their arms raised defensively as if I were about to shoot them.

"Who are you?" I asked, keeping my own voice steady.

"I'm Jeff and this is my wife, Carla, and our daughter, Stephanie."

"What are you doing here? Are you part of the bandit gang?"

His face turned ashen. "What? Bandits? No, we live here. We've lived here ever since…since…" He tried to hold back tears but began to sob. "Since those zombies have been killing people. We don't want to die. Please. Please."

Lucy leaned over the counter to look at them. "You live here alone? In this building?"

He shook his head. "Not alone. There are more of us." He pointed to the darkness that led deeper into the building.

I turned and aimed my flashlight in that direction. "I don't see anyone there."

"They're hiding," he said. "We don't want to die. None of us want to die."

I looked to Tanya for guidance. She just shrugged.

"Are you telling me you've been living here since the outbreak?" I asked Jeff.

He nodded. "We were here when it all started. We'd been on holiday in Scotland and we were driving home. Stephanie wanted to use the bathroom so we stopped here. Then it came on the news about the...the zombies. Most people left so they could get home but some of us stayed. We locked the doors and turned off the lights. We didn't want to go out there." He whimpered and added, "Don't make us go out there."

"I'm not going to make you do anything," I said. "We came here for food and water."

"We have food," he said. "And water. Please take it and leave here."

"We went into the shop," I said. "There's nothing left."

"Not there. We moved it. We live at the back of the building. In McDonald's."

"There are places you can go," I said. "The army has camps for people like you. We're heading for one right now. If you or anyone else wants to follow us in your cars…"

"No," Jeff said. "We don't want to go out there. Not until everything is back to the way it was before."

"You're going to run out of food in here eventually," Lucy said. "You should come with us."

"No," Carla said. "We don't want to. Please don't make us."

"I'm not going to make you do anything," I said again. "But I think that if you stay here, you won't last much longer."

They didn't reply.

Sam put an arm on my shoulder. "Come on, man. There's nothing we can do for these people if they don't want to be helped."

"Yeah." I backed away from the counter. "Let's go."

We went back to the main doors and I waited while the others climbed through the broken frame. I shone my flashlight into the darkness and saw more people back there. There must have been a dozen families. They all looked malnourished, pale, and frightened.

I turned to the door and climbed through. Outside, the fresh air tasted good compared to the staleness of the building, and the even the cold rain was welcome as it lashed against my face.

We walked back to the Mastiff and climbed inside.

"How terrible," Lucy said after we had closed the doors. "They're going to die in there because they're too afraid to leave."

"Fear is a powerful thing," I said.

Sam started the engine and gunned it a couple of times. "Let's get some gas." He drove out of the car park, past the cars that we now knew belonged to the families inside the services. The petrol station was situated on the exit road. The lights were on and the pumps seemed to be operational.

When we pulled up to the diesel pump, I could see the undead ambling about inside the store. There were two vehicles -a maroon Ford Focus and a blue Toyota Corolla- parked at the pumps but nobody was inside either vehicle.

Unlike the main building, the petrol station's shop hadn't been looted. I could see food on the shelves and the fridges with drinks were lit and stocked.

"Jackpot," Sam said.

I counted eight zombies inside. They moved slowly among the aisles of snacks and magazines.

"What's the plan?" I asked.

"Simple," Sam said. "We go in there, kill the zombies and turn on the gas pump. We get as much food and drink as we can carry and then we get the hell out of here. The best plans are the simplest ones."

"Okay," I said. "Sounds easy when you put it like that."

"It is easy," he said, opening his door. "I'll sort the fuel out while you guys grab the food and drink. Oh, and kill the zombies." He grinned and got out of the vehicle.

"We just kill the zombies and get the food and drink," I said to Lucy. "Simple."

"Simple," she repeated, opening the rear door.

I climbed out and stood in the bright lights by the pumps. The rain bounced off the metal canopy that hung over the pump area, keeping us dry.

As we walked toward the shop, I felt the hairs on the back of my neck rising.

Sam had said that the best plans were the simplest.

But I had learned from experience that even the simplest plans could very easily go wrong.

CHAPTER 20

WE MOVED FROM THE MASTIFF to the shop door in the same formation we had adopted at the main building. The automatic glass door that led into the shop was wedged open by what looked like a body. As we got closer, I could see that it was the body of a balding man in his fifties dressed in a shirt and tie. The back of his head and white shirt were covered in dried blood. I wondered if his car was the Ford or the Toyota.

The zombie closest to the door was a blonde woman wearing the uniform of the company that owned the petrol station. A bite on her left shoulder was oozing dark blood and, judging by the amount of blood covering the uniform, had been doing so for some time.

She moaned and lurched toward us, arms outstretched. Sam put a bullet into her brain and she dropped like a rag doll, hitting the floor with a sickening, meaty slap.

The sound alerted the other zombies. They came down the aisles and began to emit the low moan that meant they had spotted prey. They were slow and easy to kill. We dispatched them quickly.

Maybe Sam's plan was going to go smoothly after all.

He went to the counter and vaulted over it, turning the pump on before vaulting back over the counter and going outside to fill the Mastiff.

Tanya, Lucy, and I grabbed a plastic basket each and went along the aisles, filling the baskets with snack food and bottles of water. When all three baskets were full, we went out to dump the contents into the Mastiff before returning to the shop for more.

It was during our second excursion along the aisles that I heard the sound of vehicles outside. Tanya and Lucy looked toward the open door at the same time I did. The noise outside sounded like a lot of vehicles approaching the petrol station.

"We need to go now," I said in a voice that was calmer than I felt.

With our half-filled baskets in hand, we ran for the Mastiff. Sam had already replaced the pump's nozzle back onto the pump and was climbing into the driver's seat.

We threw our baskets in through the vehicle's rear door and climbed in after them. Even before I had managed to pull the door shut, Sam had floored the accelerator, taking us quickly along the road that led back to the motorway.

"Bandits?" Lucy asked as we reached the motorway.

Sam shook his head. "I think they were military vehicles." He pulled into the center lane of the motorway to avoid a group of abandoned cars.

"Guys, we're not supposed to be running from the military," I said. "We're going to a camp, remember? We work for the MoD."

Sam let out a sigh of relief. "Oh yeah, I forgot."

Everyone laughed. It was a natural release of the tension that had built inside us as soon as we had heard the vehicles. We were so used to running from everyone, including the army, that it was difficult to shake the mild paranoia that pervaded our worldview.

Sam took his foot off the gas, dropping our speed. He maneuvered around more abandoned vehicles, some of them sitting in the middle of the road.

"There's a lot of traffic today," he said lightly.

Tanya checked the map. "We're approaching Carlisle, a fairly small city. This motorway becomes the M6 and it runs right along the edge of the city."

That made me nervous. I could only imagine what a city would be like, how many thousands of zombies there must be walking the streets.

"Maybe we should take a different route," I suggested.

"No can do, man," Sam said. "This is the most direct way to get to the camp. As long as....oh, shit." He applied the brakes, bringing us to a stop.

"What is it?" I asked, moving forward so I could see out of the windows.

Ahead, a bridge spanned the motorway. Next to it, a blue sign announced WELCOME TO ENGLAND and displayed the cross of St. George flag.

Beneath the bridge, a group of cars had been parked so that they blocked all the lanes on both sides of the motorway.

"Roadblock," Sam said.

CHAPTER 21

W E WAITED, SITTING IN THE middle of the motorway with the engine running. Sam whispered, "I'm ready to slam us into reverse and get out of here."

Nothing happened. Nobody appeared on the bridge, which would be the best place for an ambush, or at the sides of the road to flank us. We simply sat there waiting for an attack that never came. Even the rain stopped, the constant pitter patter on the vehicle giving way to an eerie silence.

"Maybe they're waiting for us to get out," I whispered.

"Or maybe there's nobody here at all," Sam said.

"Only one way to find out," Tanya said. She opened her door and slid out onto the road, M16 in hand.

Still no movement from the bridge.

"Nothing," Tanya said from outside. "We need to move those cars."

We all got out of the Mastiff, but I noticed that Sam didn't turn off the engine. The big vehicle rumbled quietly while we approached the bridge and the cars parked beneath.

The surface of the road was wet and our boots splashed through rainbow-colored oil stains that floated on the puddles. There was a slight smell of rotting meat hanging in the air.

"Anyone else smell zombies?" Tanya asked, looking around for signs of trouble.

"Yeah," I said. "But I think it might be coming from the city. If there's a huge zombie population there, the smell would be noticeable from miles away."

"Okay," she said, nodding but still checking in all directions. She and Lucy stayed close to the Mastiff, keeping an eye on our surroundings while Sam and I walked into the shadows under the bridge.

The cars were parked at angles so they blocked all three lanes. Sam went up to a white Nova that blocked the middle lane and peered in through the driver's-side window. He tried the door. It opened.

Sam took the Leatherman tool from his pocket and leaned below the steering column. After a couple of minutes, the car started. Sam climbed into the driver's seat and reversed the Nova to the side of the road.

"Where did you learn to hot-wire a car?" I asked him as he came back to the roadblock and went to work on the next car in the line, a silver Honda.

"You pick things up here and there," he said. He got the Honda started and parked it next to the Nova by the side of the road.

He moved to the next car, an old Ford Fiesta, and opened it. A sudden movement inside the car made Sam step back, surprised. "Shit!" He reached for his handgun but the zombie was already clawing at his legs, pulling him down onto the road.

They rolled in the oily water, locked together by the zombie's arms and legs, which were wrapped around Sam's torso. I fumbled the Walther out of its holster and ran over to where they were struggling against each other.

The zombie's head shot forward and it sank its teeth into Sam's upper arm. Sam cried out in pain.

I reached them and put the muzzle of the Walther against the zombie's temple, squeezing the trigger as soon as I knew I wouldn't miss. The shot rang out and the bullet passed through the zombie's head, taking blood and brain matter with it as it exited through the other side of the creature's skull.

The zombie collapsed. Sam pushed it away and scrambled to his feet, holding the bleeding wound in his arm. His combat jacket was ripped and blood was oozing out of the wound and staining the camouflage-patterned fabric.

Sam's face was a grimace, his skin almost white. His eyes were glazed.

Tanya ran over and helped me support his weight as we led him back to the Mastiff. Lucy remained on guard. I could see worry in her face.

We got Sam into the back of the Mastiff. He lay on the steel floor, breathing heavily, still clutching his wound.

Tanya got the first-aid kit from beneath the passenger seat and opened it, tipping the contents out onto the floor. She grabbed a bandage and disinfectant.

"Get his jacket off," she told me.

I began to pull at the jacket but Sam batted my hand away. "I can do it myself," he said, his voice thin. He struggled out of the jacket and his T-shirt. The bite mark in his arm was a jagged red line just below his shoulder. It was still bleeding.

"I think he needs stitches," I told Tanya.

She swept her hand through the first-aid items on the floor and held up a white packet. "We'll use these. Skin closure strips."

She opened the bottle of disinfectant and poured it onto the wound. Sam gritted his teeth as the brown liquid entered the rip in his flesh.

"Hold the wound together," Tanya said.

I used my fingers to press the sides of the tear together while Tanya applied the skin closure strips. Then she cleaned the area with sterile wipes.

The skin around the bite was red and inflamed. The inflammation seemed to be spreading down the arm and over Sam's shoulder and chest.

Tanya and I looked at each other, both of us thinking the same thing. "Now we'll see if the vaccine really works," she said.

I nodded. "I hope it…"

My words were cut off by the sound of gunshots outside.

CHAPTER 22

ULLETS BEGAN RICOCHETING OFF THE safety cage. Lucy appeared at the rear of the Mastiff and said, "We need to get out of here, *now*." She climbed inside and closed the door.

"What's happening?" Tanya asked her.

"People on the bridge. They've got guns."

Tanya went up front and climbed into the driver's seat. "We're getting out of here." We began to reverse back along the motorway. Now I could see the shooters on the bridge. There looked to be maybe six or seven of them. They were all men as far as I could make out and they were dressed in civilian clothing.

"More bandits?" I asked Tanya as I got into the passenger seat up front.

"Looks like it." Her eyes roamed over the dashboard as she tried to familiarize herself with the Mastiff's controls.

There were more switches and buttons than in a conventional car but that was to be expected when the vehicle had on-board computer systems, cameras, and weapons.

"What are we going to do?" I asked her. Sam had moved two of the cars out of our way but the Ford Fiesta remained.

"We'll go through it," she said, taking the Mastiff out of reverse.

"Can't we go back up the motorway and find a way around…?"

"We can't go back," she said, shaking her head.

"Why not?"

"Look in the mirror."

I checked the side mirror. Behind us, a fleet of maybe a dozen cars was bearing down on us.

Tanya gripped the wheel tightly and hit the gas. We accelerated toward the bridge. The shooters began shooting again. Bullets careened off the front of the Mastiff. Our speed increased.

I turned in my seat and said to Lucy and Sam, "Hold on."

Lucy nodded. She and Sam were harnessed into their seats. Sam gave me a weak thumbs-up.

Everything became dark momentarily as we drove beneath the bridge. Then we slammed into the Fiesta, pushing it along the road in front of us. Its tires squealed against the wet road surface as we emerged on the other side of the bridge and into daylight.

Tanya hit the brakes, reversed slightly, and then guided the Mastiff around the crushed Fiesta. As soon as we were clear, she accelerated along the center lane, leaving the bridge behind us.

I checked the mirror again. The cars were still coming.

If it came down to a firefight on the motorway a second time, I wasn't sure we would come out on top again. There were at least twelve cars behind us and we had a man down. I wasn't even sure we had enough ammo left to take out all those vehicles.

"Can't we go any faster?" I asked Tanya.

She shook her head. "The top speed seems to be around sixty."

I felt my heart sink. Those cars could outrun us easily. They would reach us in the next couple of minutes, if not sooner.

I climbed out of my seat and went into the rear compartment to check my weapons. Lucy unharnessed herself and did the same.

"What's the best way to do this?" I asked her. "From the roof or through the rear door?"

"Both," she said. "You take the roof, I'll take the door."

"Okay." I stepped up onto the platform and opened the top hatch. The wind resistance battered me as I climbed up through the hatch, staying low, and thankful for the raised edge that ran around the perimeter of the roof. I crawled to the rear section and peered over the raised edge.

The cars were close. Nobody was shooting yet but I could see that the occupants had guns. Unlike the bandits we had seen earlier, these seemed to have a plan, and that was scarier than if they'd just started firing haphazardly at us.

I positioned my M16 so that the muzzle jutted over the edge of the roof. If we were going to go down, at least we were going to go down fighting.

Then something on the opposite side of the motorway caught my attention. There was an exit road there and coming down it was a convoy of military Jeeps. I counted five of them, painted in desert colors like the Mastiff. Each Jeep had a driver and a soldier manning a large gun mounted on the rear of the vehicle.

They came racing south along the northbound lanes and opened fire on the cars behind us, shooting across the median and over the safety barrier.

The air became thick with smoke as the fleet of cars took hits from the large-caliber guns. The scene behind us was one of mayhem as vehicles exploded and crashed. I saw a red Ford Galaxy drive off the road with black smoke pouring out of its engine, its bodywork shredded.

I crawled backward to the hatch and dropped down into the rear compartment. Lucy had the rear door open and was watching the carnage on the motorway. She turned to me and grinned. "Here comes the cavalry to save the day."

Even Sam was smiling although he looked exhausted.

The cars that had been chasing us were now no more than burning pieces of wreckage on the motorway.

The Jeeps came alongside us on the opposite side of the road and the lead driver waved his hand in a downward motion at Tanya.

"He wants us to stop," she said. "Should I?"

"After what they did to those cars, I don't think we have a choice," I answered.

She slowed us down to a gentle stop. Lucy and I got out. The road surface was beginning to dry in the midday sun now. The rotting meat smell still hung in the air.

The Jeeps halted on the other side of the barrier and three soldiers walked across to us while the others remained with their vehicles. The big guns were trained on us now. These soldiers might have saved our lives but they still didn't know who we were and they were probably ready to kill us at a moment's notice.

Tanya came around the side of the Mastiff to join us. She had kept the engine running.

The man in the lead looked to be in his late thirties. He had dark hair with some gray at the temples and a thin, hawkish face. As he got nearer to us, his eyes roamed over the Mastiff, Lucy and me, and our combat clothing. I guessed that he was probably trying to mentally process how two people who were obviously not military personnel were riding in an expensive piece of military hardware.

I was wrong. He seemed to know exactly who we were. "I was told you lot were resourceful," he said, "but where the bloody hell did you get this?" He pointed at the Mastiff.

"You know who we are?" Lucy asked.

"I think so," he said. "You should have ID badges to show me if you are who I think you are."

We dug into our pockets and showed him our badges. He inspected them and nodded before handing them back to us.

"I'm Captain Price," he said. "We were told at Prometheus that you were coming. The brigadier sent us to meet you. It seems you had a welcoming committee of undesirables so we arrived just in time."

"We were about to deal with them ourselves," Tanya said.

He looked at her and raised an eyebrow. "Yes, I'm sure you were."

Then he walked to the rear of the Mastiff and looked inside, raising an eyebrow when he saw Sam.

Price turned to face us again. "So tell me," he said, "where the bloody hell is the vaccine?"

CHAPTER 23

E TOLD PRICE ABOUT THE drones patrolling the coastline and the vaccine on our boats. He listened to our story of how we had commandeered the Mastiff and driven south on the motorway to get to Prometheus. He listened quietly and nodded when we were done.

He pointed at Sam, who was sitting in his seat quietly, his face pale and sweaty.

"And what's wrong with this chap?" Price asked.

"He's been bitten," I said.

"I see. And I assume he's already been vaccinated?"

"Yes, we all have."

Price went to the rear door and looked in at Sam. "I suppose this is as good a test as any for the efficacy of the vaccine. I'm going to have to insist that you keep him in that harness until we get to Prometheus."

"Prometheus?" Tanya said. "We just told you that the vaccine is on our boats. Call off the drones so we can go back and get it."

Price pursed his lips, thinking. "That's not my decision to make. Besides, the brigadier will want to see you. He'll decide what happens regarding the vaccine and how we get it off your boats."

He paused as if considering something and then said, "We were told that you lot might know something about a problem we've been having at the camp. Something has been sneaking in at night and attacking our men. We've had a lot of good soldiers go missing."

"Why would we know anything about that?" I asked.

"Because the men who went missing are probably the lucky ones. It's what happened to the others that you might know something about. They were killed." He paused and then added, "And their spines were torn out."

I felt Lucy stiffen next to me. My heart began to race. Was Jax at Camp Prometheus? In a way, it made sense. She had jumped overboard near the coast north of here. Camp Prometheus was the closest place that was densely-populated with living people. She must have been attracted to it like a fox attracted to a henhouse.

"I can see from your faces that you know what I'm talking about," Price said. "We were told that the creature is something to do with you people."

"She was one of us," Tanya said, her voice sad as she remembered her friend.

"Yes, so I gathered," Price said. "I also heard that you faced one of these creatures before, at a lab in Scotland."

I nodded. "We did."

"Well then, you might have some ideas about how we can get rid of this one. We'll escort you to the camp. It's a good seventy miles south of here and involves a little jaunt past Carlisle. If you're interested in zombies, you'll see plenty on that leg of our journey." He turned to go back to the Jeeps but stopped, seemingly remembering something. Turning to face us again, he pointed at Sam and said, "And keep a close eye on him."

With that, he turned and marched back to the Jeeps with his two companions.

"I can't believe Jax is here," Tanya whispered to me as we watched Price return to his vehicle.

"And I don't know why he thinks we'll know how to deal with her," I said. "We didn't exactly deal with Vess."

"Let's just get to the camp and convince this brigadier person to call off the drones," Lucy said. "As soon as they do that, we can get back to the boats."

We got back into the Mastiff. Lucy sat in the back with Sam while I went up front with Tanya.

Survivor Radio seemed to have a new presenter for the midday slot, a man named Chris Barnes. He wasn't quite as upbeat as Sasha Green had been earlier but his voice was soothing with a low Scottish burr. "This one is for all you survivors out there," he said. "Chasing Cars" by Snow Patrol began to play.

We set off down the road with the Jeeps matching our speed on the opposite side of the motorway.

"Do you trust them?" Tanya asked me.

"No, I don't. I'm grateful to them for saving us back there, and I respect the job they do, but I don't trust them. There are very few people I trust in this world. I've always been that way."

She said, "Yeah, I know what you mean," but she didn't elaborate.

A blue sign overhead told us that the motorway had become the M6 and we had fifteen miles to go before we hit the city of Carlisle.

At our current speed, that would take us about twenty minutes.

I turned in my seat to face Lucy. "How are things back there?"

"Fine," she said.

Sam attempted a grin but it looked more like a grimace. I gave him a thumbs-up and turned to face front again. I had thought, maybe naively, that being vaccinated meant a zombie bite wouldn't affect us at all. Now that I thought about it, that had been a simplistic view.

A zombie bite passed the virus into the bloodstream of the victim. That virus was deadly to an unvaccinated human so of course it wasn't going to be painless, even for a vaccinated person. A chemical reaction must be taking place in Sam's body as his vaccinated blood fought the powerful virus.

161

I just hoped it wouldn't be too long before Sam's body started to win the fight.

Twenty minutes later, we reached the junction where a slip road led to Carlisle. There were plenty of abandoned vehicles here and I could see zombies through some of the windows. Tanya steered us around them expertly and said, "I wonder how long they're going to stay trapped in those steel coffins?"

I shrugged. "Probably until they rot away or someone comes to dispatch them."

In the distance, beyond the fields and trees, I could see some of the buildings that were part of the city. A column of black smoke was rising from somewhere in that direction, obscuring the view. I wondered if there was a single living soul in any of those buildings. Probably not. And if there was, they were as good as dead.

"I wonder how they're going to clear the cities," I said. "We can vaccinate every living person in the country but someone is going to have to get rid of all the zombies that are already here. What about the cities? How many tens of thousands of undead must there be here, in this small city, never mind densely-populated places like Birmingham and London?"

"Maybe they won't ever clear everything," Tanya said. "Maybe this is what life is going to be like from now on."

That surprised me. Tanya had always been adamant that the rest of the world was uninfected. Had she changed her mind now?

The Jeeps were now on our side of the motorway. They had taken the exit at the northbound junction and turned around to join the southbound lanes. They stayed at a constant distance behind us.

"Price said we would see plenty of zombies here," Tanya said, "but I haven't seen…" Her words trailed off as she gazed at the road ahead.

I followed her gaze. The motorway was seething with zombies. They were shambling up and down the road while others staggered across the fields. Their movement seemed to have no purpose but when they heard and saw our vehicles, they began to come our way. The moan that came from so many rotted throats filled the air.

"I don't think we can drive through them," Tanya said. "There are too many." She brought us to a stop.

Price's Jeep pulled up alongside us and he motioned for Tanya to lower her window. She did and the rotten stench that entered the Mastiff was almost overwhelming. "We'll clear a path," Price said. "But you have to stick right behind us. The blue bastards will fill in any hole we make in no time. Got it?"

Tanya nodded and put the window back up quickly.

The Jeeps pulled in front of us and started to fire the big guns into the center of the zombie mass. The undead were blown apart and the Jeeps edged forward, still firing.

Tanya accelerated so that we were directly behind the Jeeps, inching our way through the horde of rotting, seething flesh. The gunners in the Jeeps continued blowing the zombies apart in front and to the sides of their vehicles and moving forward. As we were the last in the line, the horde closed in around the rear of the Mastiff and banged on the door with their fists.

At least these slow zombies wouldn't climb aboard like the hybrids had. Instead, they pounded on the steel cage to no avail. They were never going to break in here.

It took us fifteen minutes to clear a path through the horde. By the time we had driven beyond the last of them, the road behind us was full of zombies again as if we had never passed through.

The Jeeps increased their speed and Tanya did likewise to keep up with them.

I relaxed a little and closed my eyes, listening to Chris Barnes play a selection of songs by Coldplay, The Killers, Bastille, and Green Day. The lyrics of those songs spoke of a world that was gone now and might never come again. Even Tanya had her doubts that this apocalypse would ever end, and that worried me. Her outlook was usually optimistic. Not in an "everything is going to be okay" with rainbows and unicorns way, but in a pragmatic and realistic way. If she was thinking that a future without zombies was doubtful, then it probably was doubtful.

I wasn't sure if I could live the rest of my life like this, constantly running and fighting and searching for the people I loved. But I had no choice. I thought of the people living at the motorway services, too scared to go outside. They might as well already be dead. Soon, when they ran out of food and were too afraid to go out and find more, they would be dead.

I might not be the most courageous person in the world, but I could never give up on life like they had. It just wasn't in my nature.

When I opened my eyes again, there were red signs that said SURVIVORS CAMP THIS WAY every mile or so.

I turned to check on Sam. He was looking much better. The color had returned to his face and he didn't look sweaty anymore. "How's it going?" I asked him.

"I'm fine, man. I felt a bit out of it earlier but I'm all good now."

"Glad to hear it," I said, feeling a sense of relief. Even though Sam had been vaccinated, there had been a niggling voice in my head telling me that he might turn.

Half an hour later, we drove past Killington Lake Motorway Services and came to a stop at a farm gate that led to a dirt road. A red sign had been erected by the gate. It said CAMP PROMETHEUS. One of Price's men opened the gate to let us through. We followed the road past a tree-lined lake. The area was surrounded by rolling hills and would probably be picturesque if not for the huge fenced camp that had been erected there.

Just like at Camp Apollo, there were guard towers and huts. Unlike Apollo, the military huts and the civilian tents were in separate fenced-off compounds. The gate to the military area was opened and we drove through.

Another thing that made this place very different to Apollo was the number of people in the compound. The place was buzzing with activity. Mechanics worked on vehicles in a large garage, a group of soldiers was engaged in some sort of briefing, listening to a female soldier who was standing in front of a whiteboard and pointing out various areas on a diagram. There were troops jogging around the compound in white tops and camo trousers, being led by a physical training instructor who was barking insults at them.

Tanya parked the Mastiff in an area that was pointed out by one of Price's men. A number of other vehicles were parked here, from civilian cars to armored personnel carriers.

We got out and stood, watching the hive of activity. The thing that caught my immediate attention was the smell of beef and gravy coming from the cookhouse.

Price waved at us over to join him. When we reached him, he said, "I'm going to take you to see the brigadier. You," he said, pointing at Sam, "are going to see the medic."

"Hey, I'm fine, man," Sam protested.

"It wasn't a suggestion," Price said. "My men will escort you there now."

Two of the soldiers stepped forward to escort Sam to the medic. I assumed that "escort" was a euphemism for "take you there, by force if necessary".

Sam complied and told us he'd see us later.

Price said, "Come on," and marched off down the wide graveled area between the huts.

I had to almost jog to keep up with his pace. He took us to a hut that had the name Brigadier James Gordon stenciled in black on the green door. Price knocked.

"Come in." The voice was strong and confident.

Price opened the door and ushered us inside. He followed us in and closed the door behind him.

The room was a simple office with a large desk.

The brigadier was in his late fifties, maybe older, but he looked fit and solid beneath his uniform, even sitting behind the desk.

Price said, "These are the people from Alpha One, Sir. Lucy Hoffmeister, Alex Harley, and Tanya Lee."

The brigadier eyed us with a questioning look. "Are you the people who were supposed to bring me a shipment of vaccine?"

"We are," Tanya said, "and we'd have it here if not for your drones on the coast. We almost got killed trying to get to our boats."

"They're not my drones," he said. "There's a kill zone being set up along the coast. It's a huge operation. We can't let the virus leave our shores so we are quarantining the country. As well as the drones, there will be a military presence on the ground eventually. We've already mobilized ground troops to most ports and even some of the larger marinas."

"Well, if you want the vaccine, you need to let us pass through the zone so that we can get to our boats," Tanya said.

The brigadier looked at her with an amused twinkle in his eyes. "Do I, indeed? And why should I do that? Marilyn MacDonald might think it's a good idea to employ civilians in military operations, but I don't agree. As far as I'm concerned, you should be in the tents with the other civvies. Leave the soldiering to properly trained soldiers."

"Sir," Price said, stepping forward, "from what Marilyn MacDonald said, this lot have…"

"Yes, yes, I know what they've done." The brigadier stood up. "I've read the report." He walked around the desk to face us, looking at each of us in turn. "According to MacDonald, you people are the dog's bollocks when it comes to going up against zombies." He looked us up and down. "Although I must say I expected something more than what I see in front of me. You all look too casual, too untidy. I don't think I've ever seen combat uniforms worn quite so sloppily."

"We're not military personnel," I reminded him.

"No, you're not," he said, pushing his face close to mine. "And that's the problem, isn't it? It doesn't matter how good MacDonald says you are, I'm in charge of Operation Wildfire and I'd rather work with military personnel than a rag-tag bunch of heroes."

"We don't have to be here," Tanya said defiantly. "We volunteered for this."

As she said it, I could feel my chance to look at the Survivor Board slipping away. If we pissed this man off too much, he would throw us out, or worse, lock us up in the camp.

He stared at Tanya for a moment before turning to Price. "Have them escorted to the cookhouse and get a meal inside them while we discuss what to do."

"Sir." Price opened the door and summoned two of his men, giving them the order to take us to the cookhouse.

As we moved to the door, the brigadier said to Tanya, "Miss Lee, whatever happens to you and your friends, you only have yourselves to blame. You want to play at being soldiers but you didn't learn the first rule of the military."

Tanya turned to face him. "Oh? What's that?"

He grinned and said, "Never volunteer for anything."

CHAPTER 24

E WERE ESCORTED TO THE cookhouse, which was like a cafeteria inside with rows of tables and a serving area where servers were dishing out food to soldiers. The smell of food in the air made my mouth water.

Our escorts stood by the exit, chatting with each other. I had the feeling we weren't allowed to leave here until either the brigadier or Price said so. Sam was brought in through the door and came over to our table.

"What did the medic say?" Tanya asked him.

"Clean bill of health, man."

"So the vaccine does work," I said. "I had my doubts."

"Hey, I never doubted it for a second." He grabbed a tray and got into the line for food. "I never felt like I was being zombified."

"And how would you know what that feels like?" Lucy asked him.

He shrugged. "I'd just know. All I felt was like I had the flu for an hour and then it passed."

We got our food, which consisted of roast beef, mashed potatoes, vegetables, and gravy, and found a table. As we ate, we told Sam about our encounter with Brigadier Gordon and how he and Price were deciding our future.

"Fuck 'em," Sam said. "If they don't want to let us go and get the vaccine, then we're out of here. I'm starting to think that volunteering to be a part of this operation was a mistake. You try to help some people and they have their heads so far up their own asses, they can't see that you're on their side."

I finished my meal and put the knife and fork down on the plate. "Don't worry, they know how valuable the new vaccine is. They'll let us go and fetch it."

Sam pointed his fork at Lucy and me. "Have you two seen the survivor database yet?"

We shook our heads.

"Make sure you get a look at it," he said. "If we're going to get thrown out of here, we might as well gain something from this stupid trip."

"They're not going to throw us out," Tanya assured him. "The brigadier is against letting us complete the mission but Price is on our side."

"Yeah, but the brigadier outranks Price," Lucy said.

Tanya shrugged. "We'll just have to wait and see what happens."

Price appeared at the door and beckoned us to follow him. He led us back to the brigadier's office.

The brigadier was sitting behind the desk again, a number of typed papers spread out in front of him. I wondered if they were the reports on us that he'd received from Marilyn MacDonald.

"Come in, come in," he said as we entered. His tone seemed lighter, more friendly. Maybe Price had convinced him that we were the right people for the job or maybe the reports had swayed the argument in our favor. Either way, I was sure we were part of Operation Wildfire again.

He leaned back in his chair. "Captain Price has put forward a strong case for allowing you to continue working on this operation. His argument and Marilyn MacDonald's reports have convinced me that putting people like you into a camp would be a waste of resources. You might not be trained but you have experience." He flicked through the pages on the desk. "A lot of it, apparently."

Looking back up at us, he said, "So tomorrow, you will return to your boats to get the vaccine."

"And we won't get shot at?" Tanya asked.

"Of course you won't. We have signal emitters that we put into our vehicles. The signal tells the drones that the vehicle is friendly. The emitters are portable; we'll put one in the Mastiff."

Sam grinned. He had probably thought the brigadier was going to confiscate Big Betty.

"You can wipe that smile off your face," the brigadier told Sam. "I may have let you back into the operation but I cannot sanction letting civilians take charge of military technology. Two of our men will be going with you, acting as crew. They will be the driver and the gunner. You four are simply passengers. Is that understood?"

I nodded. Sam's face had fallen but he murmured a low, "Yeah."

The brigadier held out his hand. "Keys, please."

Sam reluctantly handed them over.

"Once you reach your boats, you will load the vaccine into the Mastiff," the brigadier said. "It's simple, really. Everyone clear on all that?"

We nodded. I didn't like the idea of having to travel with two soldiers; it felt like we weren't trusted to operate on our own, despite the fact that we had come this far without any help.

"Before we go," I said, "I'd like to see the survivor database."

"So would I," Lucy added.

The brigadier hesitated for a moment, thinking. He pushed a sheet of paper and a pen across the desk to us. "Write the names of the people you want to find on there. I'll have someone look them up."

"And you'll tell us the results before we leave tomorrow?" I asked.

"I'll tell you the results when you deliver the vaccine," he said.

I clenched my fists. Why was it that every time I did something for the military, they had some sort of hold over me?

I wrote Joe's name, and the names of my parents on the paper. Lucy added the names of her parents and we turned to leave.

"Just one more thing," the brigadier said.

We turned to face him.

"Good luck," he said.

CHAPTER 25

WE SPENT THE NIGHT IN a hut that Price gave us the key to. The furnishings inside were nothing more than a row of six beds but that was enough. After spending the previous night sleeping in the back of the Mastiff, the basic beds in the hut felt luxuriously comfortable.

I was awoken the next morning by the general hubbub of the camp. Sam, Tanya, and Lucy were already awake.

"Something's happening out there, man," Sam said.

The morning was wet, cold, and rainy as we stepped out of the hut. A group of soldiers stood by a section of the perimeter fence that backed onto the woods. They seemed to be having a heated discussion.

Price appeared, marching toward the assembly.

"What's happened?" I asked Price as he passed us.

"Another attack," he said, sighing. "It happens every bloody night."

We followed them to the fence. When I saw what was there, I was glad I hadn't eaten breakfast.

Four corpses hung from the wire fence. Their faces were wide-eyed, their mouths open, as if they were silently screaming. A trail of blood and gore stained the fence behind each man as it dripped from the tear in their bodies where their spines had once been.

Price turned to a soldier who was holding a clipboard. "Is anyone missing?"

"Yes, Sir," the soldier replied. "Seven men went missing last night."

Price shook his head in disgust. "Why is it doing this?" he murmured. Then he said, "Get those bodies down now," and turned on his heels before marching back toward the huts.

As he passed us, he said, "Come with me."

We followed him to a hut with his name on the door: Captain Colin price. Inside, the office was identical to the brigadier's except the desk wasn't as large. Price seemed to deflate as soon as he entered and was out of sight of his men. His shoulders dropped and a weakness seemed to enter his eyes. "I don't know what to do," he said. "It's like this every night. Some of our soldiers are killed while others go missing. It never attacks the civilian camp, only this compound."

"By 'it', I think you mean Jax," Tanya said.

"Yes, Jax. Your friend. Well, ex-friend, I suppose. I'm sure she wouldn't think twice before killing all of you now that she's become this…"—he consulted a typed report on his desk—"…Type 1. Or whatever the hell those eggheads at Apocalypse Island call it."

"Type 1," I said. "There are only two of them in existence, Jax and Vess. Vess is patient zero."

"You faced Vess," Price said. "So tell me, how do we defeat Jax? We can't have good soldiers being torn to pieces or going missing every bloody night."

"We faced him but we didn't defeat him," I said. "When we left Site Alpha Two, Vess was still in the building and very much alive as far as I know. The soldiers there were fighting him."

He waved his hands dismissively. "No, that all went tits up. After a wave of zombies came out of the building, the soldiers sealed the place, deciding it was better to lock Vess up in there than go in and try to kill him. Too dangerous."

Tanya stepped in. "Either way, we had no idea how to deal with Vess then and we don't know how to stop Jax now."

"But there is one thing we can warn you about," I said. "The Type 1's are just as intelligent as they were before they became infected. They don't become mindless killing machines like the zombies, or rage-driven murderers like the hybrids. They can calculate and plan. So be careful."

177

"Right," he said sarcastically. "Great advice. 'Be careful'. I'm sure that's going to save my men from being torn apart by that monster." He marched to the door, straightening his posture before opening it. "Come on, it's time for you to go and collect that vaccine."

We followed him past the huts to the area where the Mastiff was parked. Two soldiers stood by the open doors of the vehicle. On the ground between them was a green-colored metal box about the size of a car battery with a black metal handle. One of the soldiers was blonde and looked like he might be nineteen years old. He was introduced to us as Thornley, the gunner.

The other soldier was black, in his thirties, and named Cooper. He was the driver.

"And this is a Magpie," Price said, indicating the metal box on the ground. "It emits a signal that tells any drones overhead that your vehicle is friendly. The old version used to be fixed to our vehicles. Now, it's portable because some of our chaps in the Middle East had to switch to local vehicles and the results weren't pleasant when the drone operators mistook them for the enemy. So any vehicle you carry the Magpie in will be friendly as far as the drones are concerned."

He patted the side of the Mastiff. "She's all fuelled up and her ammo has been replenished. You shouldn't have any trouble getting to the coast but I've arranged a convoy to escort you as far as Carlisle. After that, you're on your own. Any questions?"

We didn't have any, so he said, "Good luck," and turned back to the huts.

"Who's riding up front with me?" Cooper asked as he climbed up into the driver's seat.

We all looked at Sam, assuming that if he wasn't allowed to drive, at least sitting in the front passenger seat would be the next best thing.

But he had already climbed in through the rear door, his face downcast.

"I think he's sulking," Tanya whispered to Lucy and me.

"I heard that," Sam said from inside the Mastiff.

Tanya rolled her eyes. "I'll ride up front if Mr. Sulky Pants doesn't want to."

"I heard that too," Sam said.

"You were supposed to," she said lightly as she went to the front of the vehicle and climbed up into the passenger seat.

Lucy and I joined Sam in the back, sitting across from him.

Thornley climbed in and placed the Magpie up near the front storage compartment. Then he opened the top hatch, donned a headset and a helmet, and took his place on the raised gunner's platform.

"Is everyone strapped in?" Cooper asked, starting the engine and putting on his own headset so that he could communicate with Thornley.

Lucy and I muttered an affirmative. Sam remained silent.

As we reversed out of the parking space, Sam asked Cooper, "Can we at least put the SDU screens on, man?"

"No need," Cooper answered. "Thornley and I are the crew. Leave the driving and shooting to us. You just sit back and enjoy the ride."

We drove out of the camp gate.

Sam looked at Lucy and me and said, "Well, this sucks."

CHAPTER 26

HEN WE REACHED THE MOTORWAY, the rain became heavier. I wondered how Thornley was enjoying it with his head sticking out through the roof hatch. The rain must be pinging off his helmet and driving him crazy.

Cooper took us south to a slip road, took it, and crossed over a bridge so that we could take the road that led to the northbound lanes. When we were back on the motorway heading north, I saw two of the Jeeps that made up our escort driving in front of us.

Sam folded his arms and looked up at the ceiling, whistling a nondescript tune. He looked like he was waiting at a doctor's office, wishing he were anywhere else but where he was right now. After ten minutes of whistling and looking as if he might actually die of boredom, he turned to Cooper and said, "Hey, man, can we have the radio on?"

Without speaking, Cooper turned on the radio.

Sam looked at me and said, "This guy's a barrel of laughs."

The Sasha Green Morning Show was on and Sasha was playing mainly eighties and nineties hits. Sam fidgeted in his seat and looked so impatient that I wouldn't be surprised if he asked Cooper, "Are we there yet?" despite the fact that we had only just begun the journey.

I leaned my head back and closed my eyes, letting the constant rumble of the Mastiff's engine lull me into a relaxed drowsiness.

I must have dozed off because the next thing I knew, we were leaving the motorway and driving toward winding narrow side roads with low stone walls and fields on either side.

"Where are we?" I asked Lucy.

"We're coming off the motorway so we can avoid that bridge where we were ambushed," she said. I blinked the tiredness out of my eyes and stretched. The rain was still falling and I was sure that Thornley must be really pissed off by now.

"What about Carlisle? Did we go past it already?"

"Yeah," Sam said. "And it was boring. The rain is keeping all the zombies indoors." His humor hadn't improved any since I'd fallen asleep.

Cooper said, "Everyone hold on tight. We've got bandits on our tail."

The top gun began firing. I hoped Thornley was as accurate with it as Tanya had been.

"How many of them are there?" I asked Cooper.

He shrugged. "Maybe six or seven cars. Don't worry, they're stuck behind us on these narrow roads. There's not much they can do here."

Thornley continued to fire. I had no idea if he was even hitting anything and it was annoying me to be sitting here helpless and kept in the dark about what was happening outside.

"Screw this," I said, unfastening my harness.

Sam saw what I was doing and grinned. He unbuckled his own harness and grabbed an M16.

"Hey, hey," Cooper shouted. "What are you doing back there? Sit down and put your harnesses back on."

Ignoring him, I switched on the SDU screen so that it showed the view behind us.

The rear tires of the Mastiff were throwing up rainwater and dirt from the road. A line of cars was sticking close to our tail.

It didn't look like Thornley had actually hit anything with the big gun. "What are you doing up there?" I shouted at him. "Firing warning shots?"

"Yes," he shouted back. "I'm showing them that they should pull back because we have superior firepower."

"You're wasting bullets, man," Sam said.

Cooper shouted. "Please sit down and let us handle this."

I could see the driver of the lead car, a bearded man with a scarred face. The man sitting next to him in the passenger seat was bald and looked like he might have been a bare-knuckle boxer in a previous life. He was holding an SA-80, the machine gun usually used by the British Army, but he wasn't firing at us.

"Why aren't they firing?" I asked Sam.

"I don't know, man."

Were they waiting for the road to widen so they could flank us? There was some reason they were biding their time.

"Tanya, do you have the map?" I asked her.

"Yeah."

"What's up ahead?"

"Nothing much. There's a crossroads about a mile from here."

"They're not firing at us because they're herding us toward the crossroads," I told Cooper. "There will be more cars there, maybe a roadblock. These guys behind us are making sure we can't go back once we see it."

"Thornley," I said. "Aim the gun ahead of us. You might want to try and hit something this or we're going to be in trouble."

Thornley spoke into his microphone. "Cooper?"

Cooper hesitated. Then he said, "Do as he says."

The gun mount whirred as Thornley turned it to face front.

Lucy had unstrapped herself and grabbed an M16. Tanya slid out of her seat and into the rear compartment. "You think there will be many of them, Alex?"

I nodded. "Yeah. If they can spare a dozen cars just to make sure we keep going forward, they must have a lot of personnel at the crossroads waiting for us."

"We should be able to storm right through them in Betty," Sam said.

"The problem will be when we get to Muldoon," I said. "Once we're at the harbor, we'll need to get out of Betty and onto a boat. That's if there are even any boats there after that drone attack."

"Well, that's the answer, man." Sam pointed at the Magpie. "As long as we've got that thing on board, the drone won't attack us. But the bandits will be toast."

He was right. If we played this the right way, the drones would take care of our bandit problem.

"Crossroads ahead," Cooper said. "There are cars everywhere. And a roadblock."

We moved forward to look through the windscreen. The bandits had parked cars on the road ahead and on the roads going left and right. There were gunmen crouched behind the cars and some in the fields.

"We're going to go through them," Cooper said. "Oh, shit, they've got an RPG."

I saw the RPG at the same time Cooper did. A man standing in a field to our right had the anti-tank weapon on his shoulder and was aiming it at us.

"Thornley, the guy in the field!" I shouted.

The top gun boomed. At the same time, the man in the field fired the RPG. He was cut to pieces by Thornley's shots but the anti-tank missile was already flying our way.

I tried to grab my seat harness to prepare for the impact but the missile hit us before I had wrapped my fingers around the material. The blast ripped into the side of the Mastiff, making a deafening bang and shaking the vehicle.

Cooper managed to keep us on the road. We shot forward into the roadblock of cars, pushing them aside. The gunmen started shooting at us.

I expected Thornley to return fire but there was no sound from the gun on the roof.

"Thornley, you okay?" I asked him.

He collapsed onto the platform. "I…no. Not okay."

Tanya grabbed the first-aid kit and rushed over to him. He leaned heavily against the wall.

"What's wrong?" Tanya asked. "Where does it hurt?"

He shook his head slowly. "It doesn't hurt. It doesn't hurt at all." He closed his eyes.

"Thornley!" Tanya said, shaking him. "Thornley!"

His body was lifeless. Tanya laid him on the floor. I could see blood seeping through his jacket at the base of his neck. He had taken a bullet at the roadblock.

I checked the SDU screen. The gunmen were getting into their cars and joining the vehicles already following us.

Tanya got up onto the platform. I expected to hear the gun fire and see cars explode behind us, but Tanya came down again. "The gun's damaged."

"Don't worry," I said. "The drones will take care of them." I went up front and climbed in next to Cooper. "How much farther to the coast?"

"We should be there in about half an hour. Is Thornley dead?"

"He is," I said.

"Damn. He was a good kid. His whole family got killed right after the zombies first appeared. He always said that he would be reunited with them one day. He was a man of faith, you know? Well, I guess he's with them now."

"Listen, I said, "when we get to the coast and get rid of these bandits, we should take the boats south instead of driving all the way back. We can find a vehicle and only have to drive fifty miles to Prometheus. That was our original plan but we had a problem with the drones. With the Magpie, we don't have that problem."

"But the captain's orders were to load the vaccine onto the Mastiff and drive it back."

"He didn't know we were going to lose Thornley and take an RPG blast. Who knows what damage it's done? If we try to drive all the way back, we might not even make it."

187

"I don't know," he said. "I follow orders. "I know you guys aren't real soldiers but I have my job to consider."

"What are they going to do? Fire you? You're a valuable resource in this apocalypse. They won't fire you just because you followed the best course of action to get the vaccine to Prometheus safely."

"I'll have to think about it."

"Of course." He had half an hour to make up his mind and it really didn't matter what he decided. I had already made up my mind that once I was on the *Easy*, I was sailing south. Driving the route to the camp had been a necessity yesterday but I was damned if I was going to leave the safety of the boat to make that drive again. I wanted Cooper to agree to my plan because that would save any conflict we might have when we got to the coast.

But if he refused and insisted on driving back, I would tell him that he'd be doing so alone. Given the choice between that or coming with us, I knew he would choose the boats. Driving back alone would be suicide.

We drove on for half an hour with the bandits in pursuit but not making their move yet. When we saw a sign for Muldoon, I told Cooper to follow it.

When the half-ruined fishing village came into sight through the rain-streaked windscreen, I directed Cooper to the barricade and told him to drive down to the beach. Maybe there was a boat in the harbor that hadn't been sunk in the drone attack.

He took us past the *Kingfisher* pub and down the road toward the sea. It looked like there were at least twenty cars behind us now. As they slowed down to drive through the gap in the barricade, a sudden flash erupted behind the lead car. The entire village seemed to shake as the cars exploded one after the other like dominoes falling.

Cooper kept his cool and got us to the harbor in one piece.

Sitting on the pebbly beach, exactly where we had left it, was the Zodiac.

We got out of the Mastiff and crossed the beach to our craft. It looked undamaged, unlike the boats that had been moored at the harbor. They lay at odd angles, grounded on the sea bed.

"Let's get out of here," Sam said, untying the Zodiac from the metal stake.

I turned to Cooper. "You really don't want to drive all the way back to the camp, do you?"

He nodded toward the *Easy* and *Escape* floating out at sea. "Have you got food on board those boats?"

"We have," I said.

"Then no, I don't want to drive back."

I grinned and slapped him on the shoulder. "If you want, you can even have steak tonight."

"I won't say no to that."

We made two trips in the Zodiac. Sam and Tanya took the snacks and drinks we had taken from the petrol station in the first run. Tanya stayed on board while Sam piloted the craft back to take Lucy, Cooper, and me as well as all the weapons and ammo. We also took the Magpie because we were going to need it when we got another vehicle farther south.

But that could wait. For now, I was glad to be heading home to *The Big Easy*.

CHAPTER 27

FTER WE HAD STOWED THE weapons and snack food, we decided to take the boats down the coast, look for a suitable place to go ashore that was as close as we could get to the road that led to Prometheus, and spend the night on the boats.

The brigadier was expecting us to be driving back today with the vaccine but as far as I was concerned, he could sweat for a while.

I climbed up to the bridge and sank into the pilot's chair, feeling instantly at home among the controls. Cooper was with Tanya and Sam on the *Escape*, which was already beginning to sail south.

Lucy was in the living area below me, either listening to the radio or reading a book. I wished the day was sunny instead of wet because then Lucy would sit on the aft deck, usually with the radio playing.

But apart from the weather, everything else was perfect. Tomorrow would bring more hardships, no doubt, but for now we were on the waves and free from the perils of the mainland.

And if all went well tomorrow and I finally discovered where Joe and our parents were, then soon they would be on board with us. Then things really would be perfect.

I hoped the brigadier would be true to his word and check the database to find my family☐.

By the time we reached the area of the coast that would give us the closest access point to Prometheus, the rain had eased a little. The radio crackled and Sam's voice said, "Dude, do you see what I see?"

I looked toward the coast. I saw an empty, sandy beach with cliffs behind it but not much else.

"Where are you looking?" I asked Sam.

"On the cliffs, man."

I looked up and saw what he was referring to. I smiled. It was perfect.

Atop the cliff was a cafe. In the car park sat a single vehicle. A bus.

"Can you drive a bus?" I asked Sam.

"Of course. Can't everyone?"

"No."

"It's easy," he said.

"Okay, you want to go check it out?"

"Nah, it'll still be there tomorrow. For now, let's just relax. Drop anchor, man, this is where we're spending the night."

I wasn't going to argue with that. I cut the engine and dropped the anchor. We had stayed a good distance from the coast because of the drones, despite the fact that the Magpie was on board the *Escape*. There was no need to fall under the scrutiny of a drone operator if we didn't have to.

I got the binoculars and aimed them at the bus on the cliffs. It was a single-decker painted in blue and white. I saw movement within and adjusted the focus on the binoculars. The bus driver was still in there, his mottled blue skin starkly contrasting with his crisp white shirt. I played the binoculars over the rest of the vehicle. The driver seemed to be the only zombie in there.

I went down to the living area and found Lucy sitting on the sofa, her legs curled up beneath her as she read a paperback romance novel. The Chris Barnes Midday Show was playing on the radio, with Bastille's "Things We Lost in the Fire" currently coming out of the speakers.

I went to the freezer and took out five steaks, setting them onto a plate on the counter so they would defrost for later.

Lucy put the book down and stretched languorously. "I'm going to go down to the bedroom and take a nap. Want to come?"

I recognized the wicked glint in her blue eyes. "Yes," I said, following her to the door. "I do."

* * *

The rest of the day passed too quickly. No sooner had Lucy and I showered and returned to the living area than it was time to prepare dinner. Sam, Tanya, and Cooper came over in their Zodiac and we ate the steaks while telling Cooper of our adventures. We learned that he was divorced and had no children. The army had always been his first love. Without it, he would be lost.

We drank a toast to Thornley before calling it a night. Sam, Tanya, and Cooper returned to the *Escape* while Lucy and I went down to bed.

It was in the early hours of the morning that I was startled awake by a nightmare. I sat up in bed and looked out of the porthole at the dark sky while I tried to rid my mind of the images that had woken me.

Lucy sat up and touched my shoulder lightly. "Are you okay?"

"Yeah, I'm fine. It was just a nightmare." I lay back down and closed my eyes, hoping that when sleep returned, it wouldn't bring the nightmare back with it.

I had dreamed that I was standing in a scorched field, surrounded by other people. In the center of the crowd was Jax, naked with her dark veins standing out in stark contrast to her skin.

She looked at me and smiled but there was no humor in that smile; it was pure evil. Then, as she stood there, black roots began to sprout from her fingertips, their tendrils twisting and reaching for the scorched earth. When the roots reached the ground, they disappeared into the soil.

Suddenly, the people around me looked down at their feet. Dark roots were growing up from the ground and twisting their sinewy tendrils around everyone's feet and legs, creeping up and up until they covered the people entirely.

The roots fell away and everyone had become a zombie. They turned to look at me with their yellow eyes.

Then they all started to stagger toward me.

CHAPTER 28

THE FOLLOWING MORNING WAS BRIGHT and sunny, the clear blue sky promising a day without rain. As we rode the Zodiac to the beach, I still had memories of the Jax nightmare running through my mind. I tried to push it out of my head. I needed to be alert if I was going to live through today and see tomorrow.

We landed on the beach and dragged the Zodiac up along the sand to the rocks at the base of the cliffs. Leaving it there, we found a set of concrete steps that climbed from the beach to the cafe above and ascended them warily. We had no idea what might be at the top of the cliffs. We knew the bus driver was a zombie and that the presence of one zombie usually indicated that there were more somewhere close by.

That was why we hadn't brought any of the vaccine boxes across with us yet; we wanted to scout the area first and make sure it was as safe as we could make it before we loaded ourselves down with boxes.

Our ammo supplies were low, so Lucy and I had elected to bring our baseball bats instead of the guns for the trip to the cafe. That also meant that we could dispatch any zombies, including the bus driver, quietly.

The bus was the only vehicle parked outside the cafe. The cafe itself looked deserted. "There's nothing in there that I can see," Lucy said, peering through the window.

We moved to the bus. The emergency exit at the rear was open. "Why didn't he get out this way?" Cooper asked.

"If there isn't something to motivate him to do that, he won't," I said. "He'll just stay in the same place until something catches his attention."

"Well, we've caught his attention now," Cooper said, pointing through the bus windows to where the driver was lurching along the aisle between the seats. He had heard us speaking and was coming this way to bite us and spread the virus.

Or so he thought.

He stumbled out of the emergency exit and onto the cement surface of the car park. He groaned when he saw us.

I smashed his head in with my bat. He fell to the ground and lay there, the wound in his head oozing dark blood.

I looked around. The area seemed to be free of any other threats.

"Let's get the vaccine," Tanya said. "I'm sure that by now the brigadier is worrying about us."

* * *

It took us over an hour to load all the boxes into the bus. By the time we were done, I felt exhausted. My lack of sleep, due to the nightmare, was catching up with me. We had checked the bus over before loading it and found the keys already in the ignition. There was enough fuel to get us to Prometheus and back.

We boarded the bus, but before sitting down in one of the front seats -the other seats were all piled high with the vaccine- I went to one of the boxes and opened it. I removed three syringes of vaccine and put them in the pocket of my combat jacket. If I was going to find Joe and my parents, I was also going to vaccinate them.

I turned to Lucy. "Do you want to take two of these in case you find your parents?"

She shook her head. She really was sure that her parents were dead.

I sat next to her and offered her a smile that didn't really mean anything but at the same time meant everything.

Sam started the bus. The engine thrummed like a heartbeat. We set off along the road that would take us to Camp Prometheus.

During the drive, we saw zombies in the fields and in the small villages we passed through, but none of them bothered us. Some of the creatures glared at us with their yellow eyes but by the time they had seen us, we were gone again. Sam kept us moving along at a steady pace.

When we reached the M6 motorway, we only had to drive down it for five miles before we reached the gate that led to Prometheus.

We drove past the lake and woods to the military compound. After the gates were opened for us and we drove into the compound, we got out of the bus, ready to go in search of the brigadier.

There was no need. He came marching over to us with a grin on his face. Seeing the cardboard boxes piled on the seats and in the aisle, he simply said, "Well done." He told Cooper to report to his squad. Cooper said goodbye to us and marched away along the street. The brigadier looked around. "I sent two men with you. Where is the other?"

"He didn't make it," Tanya said.

"Fine," the brigadier said coldly. "Now, I have something to show you."

"Wait," I said. "Before you show me anything, I want to see the results of the database search for my family."

He sighed, obviously frustrated by my demand. But the truth was, I couldn't wait any longer to find out if my family was still alive. I had to know now.

He took a slip of paper from his pocket. Before speaking to me, he addressed Lucy. "We searched for your parents on the Board. Unfortunately, their names aren't in there. Of course, that only means that they haven't come into a camp. It doesn't mean that they aren't alive."

"Yes, it does," Lucy said.

Price turned to me. "Your family is currently at this location." He handed me the slip of paper. I read the words written on it: Camp Achilles. Brecon Beacons. Wales.

"You're kidding," I said. "The Brecon Beacons is where I was when this all started. And now you're saying that Joe and my parents are at a camp there?"

He nodded. "They've been at that camp for the past two weeks. The camp they were at previously was attacked. It's not really much of a coincidence; the camps are usually built at remote locations so the Brecon Beacons is perfect. Lovely views if you like mountains."

I doubted Joe was enjoying the view from within a locked compound.

"Anyway, that's done now," the brigadier said, cutting in. "You delivered the vaccine and I told you where your family is. Now, come with me to the lab." He began walking and we followed.

"I remember telling you," he said, "that trained military personnel are the best type of people suited to these missions. Civilians, no matter how skilled, will never be able to match a trained soldier."

"That is what you said, and we didn't disagree," I told him.

"No, you didn't disagree, but I could tell that you lot thought you were superior to me and my men."

I had no idea where he had gotten that impression. He must have an inferiority complex because we had never said that.

"I've proved you wrong," he said. "Last night, my men achieved what you couldn't."

"It's not a competition," I said.

"Oh, but of course it is. Life is a competition, my boy. I let you carry out this mission partly because Marilyn MacDonald sent me glowing reports about your actions at Site Alpha Two. You faced a Type 1 and lived to tell the tale."

I had no idea where he was going with this so I kept my mouth shut.

"Do you think your actions were so noteworthy?" he asked. "I mean, you didn't capture Vess, did you?"

"No, we didn't capture him," I said. "We tried to kill him. We couldn't." I remembered Johnny shooting Vess but the creature being so fast that it dodged the bullet.

We reached a long hut that was the lab, according to the stenciled letters on the door.

The brigadier opened the door and ushered us inside. "It doesn't matter how highly Marilyn MacDonald speaks of you. You faced a Type 1 but you couldn't kill it or capture it. My men, on the other hand, managed to capture this last night." He pointed along the length of the lab.

It was like the building we had seen at Camp Apollo. There were less stainless steel tables here, though, and none of them held corpses. Halfway along the room was a Plexiglas cell, exactly like the one at Apollo.

Except this one had an occupant.

I looked at the naked female form imprisoned in the Plexiglas cube. I could hardly believe who it was.

CHAPTER 29

ANYA RUSHED TO THE PLEXIGLAS cell to see her friend. Jax stood motionless, showing no emotion in her yellow eyes when Tanya said her name. Jax looked strong and sleek, her darkly-veined skin taut over her muscles. She looked at Tanya with a blank stare.

"She doesn't recognize me," Tanya said.

"I think she does." I walked up to the Plexiglas and looked in at Jax. She regarded me with the same emotionless stare. "She just doesn't attach any emotion to us." I was sure that she did know who we were. As I had told the brigadier before, Type 1s were intelligent.

"We set a trap last night," he said, 'and she walked right into it. We waited for her to come over the fence and trapped her in nets. It was a big operation because we had to cover every possible entry point. But we got her.''

"What are you going to do with her?" Tanya asked, with tears in her eyes. It was obvious that even though Jax had no feelings toward Tanya anymore, that situation wasn't reciprocal.

I felt the same way as Tanya. Jax was a monster now, a creature capable of spreading the virus and also killing viciously, but she had once been our friend. I knew that she should die before she did any more damage to humanity, but I didn't want her to suffer.

"Our scientists will study her," the brigadier said. "As you said, the Type 1 creatures are strong and intelligent. They are infected with a pure strain of the virus. Just think of the uses we could put that to if we managed to recreate it in a lab.

"This country has suffered a tragedy with the outbreak of the zombies. But we can turn that tragedy to our advantage. We will have something that no other country has: a virus capable of inducing a killer instinct fed by fearlessness, and ferocity."

"You want to weaponize it?" Lucy asked.

"We are going to explore the military applications," he said.

"He wants to weaponize it," Sam said.

The brigadier looked at him sharply. "You make it sound as if I'm working on my own initiative. We've been ordered to study the creature and those orders have come down from the highest ranking military officials in our government."

Sam shook his head slowly in disbelief. "You really need to watch a movie or two, man. You'd realize that this isn't going to end well for anybody."

Something didn't seem right. I had seen how Vess had managed to avoid capture at Alpha Two, how he had been impossible to kill. Why should Jax, who was the same type of creature -intelligent and cunning- allow herself to be captured by a bunch of soldiers with nets?

Was that it? Had she allowed herself to be captured?

I looked at her as she stood placidly in the Plexiglas prison and felt an icy finger creep up my spine. "She let you capture her," I said.

"What?" The brigadier looked furious. His face flushed an angry purple. He had brought us in here to gloat about his achievement of catching Jax, but now I was telling him that his achievement meant nothing, that he had been fooled by the creature he'd thought he'd captured. "Don't be absurd!"

"I told you the Type 1s are just as intelligent as they were before they were turned. Jax knew that we were part of the mission to develop the new vaccine because she was at Site Alpha Two with us when we went to get the H1NZ1.

"She probably watches the camp in the daytime from the woods by the fence. When she saw us arrive here yesterday, she must have guessed that we were bringing the vaccine. That's why she allowed herself to be caught by your men."

"What do you mean. Alex?" Lucy looked worried.

"These labs are under constant guard," I said. "Jax let herself be caught because she wanted to get in here. She wants to destroy the vaccine."

"Listen to yourself," the brigadier said. "What you're saying is crazy. She's in the lab, but she's in a cell. What good is that going to do her?"

I looked at the Plexiglas surrounding Jax. "Maybe she made a mistake," I said, "and she didn't know you were going to put her somewhere she couldn't escape from. Or maybe she knows this cell can't hold her."

Suddenly, I wanted to get out of the lab as quickly as possible. "We need to leave," I said to the others. To the brigadier, I said, "You need to make sure the vaccine is protected. If Jax can get out of here…"

I stopped when I heard shouts and gunshots outside.

The brigadier looked toward the door. "What the bloody hell is going on out there?" He pulled the door open and bellowed, "What's happening? I want a situation report now, damn it!"

"We're under attack," someone shouted.

The brigadier stormed out of the lab but not before ordering us to go with him. We followed him outside, and I felt glad to be away from Jax. I glanced over at Lab 3 where the vaccine was stored. There was no one guarding that hut specifically.

Captain Price rushed over to us and spoke to the brigadier. "Sir, there's a horde of hybrids in the northern quadrant. They've broken through the perimeter fence."

"Have you mobilized the men?"

"Yes, Sir. All available personnel have been mobilized to the area and are dealing with the situation."

"All right." The brigadier seemed to calm down slightly after being given this information but I felt even more nervous. It was too much of a coincidence that the hybrids were attacking at the same time that Jax was in the lab. I didn't like this at all. Everyone in the camp was focused on the hybrid attack. There was nobody in this area other than the guards on the fence and in the towers.

The brigadier beckoned over two of the soldiers who were patrolling the inner fence. "Coleman and Simpson," he said, reading their name badges, "I want you to go into Lab 1 and guard the prisoner in there."

They nodded and said, "Yes, Sir," before marching over to the lab where Jax was being held.

"See?" the brigadier said, turning to face me. "Don't ever say I never listen to you."

"If she can get out of that plastic cage," Tanya said, "two men won't make a difference."

"That cell is strong enough to hold an elephant," he said. "Now, are you going to come and see how my soldiers deal with hybrids or will you just tell me the hybrids allowed themselves to be killed?" He chuckled to himself and marched toward the northern quadrant with Price.

"That guy is an asshole," Sam said, watching the two officers disappear from sight.

"I think we should get our guns from the bus," I said. "I've got a really bad feeling about this."

"I know what you mean," Tanya said. "It feels like the hybrid attack is a distraction."

"Yeah," I agreed. "Let's get the guns and come back here. If Jax is going to go for the vaccine, we have to stop her."

"You really think she's going to do that?" Lucy asked as we made our way to the bus.

"Even if she isn't, there's no harm in us guarding the vaccine. The soldiers in these towers are focused on guarding the labs against attacks from the outside, not from within the labs themselves."

From the north, shots rang out and screams cut through the air. Things weren't going as well as the brigadier had hoped. We ran for the bus. If the soldiers couldn't keep the hybrids at bay, the creatures would be here soon. We needed the M16s. If we had to hold off a horde of hybrids with only the Walther PPKs, we didn't stand a chance.

As we approached the bus, I halted and said, "Wait, something's wrong."

Everyone stopped and looked at me. "What is it?" Tanya asked.

I pointed to the guard towers by the gate. "Where are the guards?"

Everyone looked at the towers that flanked the main gate. They were empty.

"They're probably helping to fight the hybrids," Lucy suggested.

"All of them?" I couldn't believe the brigadier would take the guards off the gate simply to add a few extra soldiers to his already-considerable number of men in the northern quadrant. "And the guards patrolling the fence, too?"

Then I saw dark, lifeless shapes lying on the ground beneath the towers and inside the fence.

We ran over to inspect the bodies.

They lay in the gravel as if they were rag dolls tossed to the ground by a bored child. Their faces still held expressions of shock and surprise.

Their spines were missing.

"What the hell?" Tanya asked. "Jax is in the lab. How did this happen?"

A figure stepped out from behind the bus and, when I saw who it was, my blood ran cold.

Vess.

CHAPTER 30

ESS STOOD BY THE BUS, watching us. He was naked and covered in blood. His yellow eyes looked at us with a hint of cruel amusement. We had failed to kill him at Site Alpha Two and now here he was to punish that failing. He stepped forward as if he had all the time in the world.

He probably did, but as soon as he reached us, our time would be over. He would kill us in the same savage manner he had killed the soldiers. I remembered when he'd torn out Johnny Drake's spine and thrown the dead body aside. If we didn't get out of here now, that same fate would befall us.

We drew our handguns and fired. Vess dodged back behind the bus with blinding speed before reappearing and running at us.

I fired two more shots, sure that I had hit him. The Walther's slide slid back, telling me the gun was empty.

The others had expended their magazines too.

And Vess was still coming.

"Run!" I shouted.

Lucy and I fled back toward the labs. Sam and Tanya went the other way, toward the car parking area.

Vess followed Lucy and me.

"What are we going to do?" Lucy gasped as we ran for the inner fence.

"The soldiers in the towers, and on patrol," I managed to say between heaving breaths. "They'll shoot at him. Maybe he won't be able to dodge the bullets. If they all fire at once."

It was our only chance of survival. But even as I said it, I didn't have much hope. There was no way Vess had dodged all our bullets a moment ago, yet he seemed unhurt by them. Was he bullet-proof?

No, that was ridiculous. I had to believe that the soldiers guarding the lab could kill him. Without that belief, I might as well stop running and let Vess catch up with me. If the soldiers couldn't stop him, we were all dead.

"Alex!" Lucy said. It came out as a whimper. She pointed at the lab compound ahead.

The soldiers lay dead within the fence. The guard towers, where we had seen soldiers no more than five minutes ago, were empty.

The door to Lab 1 was open.

So was the door to Lab 2. Jax had gotten within the compound by letting the brigadier capture her, but she didn't know exactly where the vaccine was being stored. She had gone to the wrong lab.

"Go to Lab 3," I told Lucy. "We'll try to barricade ourselves in."

Vess was still chasing us but I had the sense that he was toying with us like a cat torturing a mouse. He could have caught us easily by now but he was biding his time. The bastard was probably enjoying this.

The gate to the lab compound was closed but it hadn't been locked before and I prayed it wasn't now.

We pushed it open and ran into the compound, heading for Lab 3.

"Is this a good idea?" Lucy asked as we reached the door. "We're leading him straight to the vaccine."

"We don't have a choice." I pushed open the door and we rushed inside. I slammed the door behind us. "Find something we can use to barricade it!"

"There's nothing here!"

The lab was empty except for the boxes of vaccine stacked at the far end of the room. They were too light to be of any use.

The door burst open and Vess stepped into the lab. His mouth twisted into a sneer when he saw that we were trapped with nowhere to go. He took a few steps toward us. Lucy and I backed away.

Jax came in through the door and stood behind Vess. Her yellow eyes regarded us with the coldness of a lizard staring at a bug.

We retreated all the way to the stack of cardboard boxes. This was as far as we could go. We were going to die here. And after we were dead, I assumed that Vess and Jax would destroy the vaccine.

Humanity's fight against the virus would be set back and while the people at Apocalypse Island rushed to make more vaccine, these two monsters would be on the loose, destroying the survivors camps. By the time they were done, there might be no one left alive. The country would be taken over by the undead.

Vess stepped toward us slowly, savoring the moment. Jax had come farther into the room. Maybe she wanted to watch us die. Maybe they were going to fight over who got which spine when we were dead.

I had nothing left to fight back with. Somewhere in my combat jacket was a Leatherman tool. It would probably be useless against Vess, but I wasn't going to just stand here and let him take us down.

Reaching into my pocket, my fingers connected with the three vaccine-loaded syringes I had taken for my family. I couldn't remember which pocket the Leatherman was in.

In desperation, I fished one of the syringes out of my pocket and opened the protective plastic tube. I slid the syringe out into my hand. I didn't think that stabbing Vess with the needle was going to do anything -the vaccine was meant to protect uninfected humans from the virus, not be injected into patient zero- but I had nothing else to try.

He reached forward and grabbed me by the throat, lifting me into the air. I couldn't breathe. With a fatalism brought on by my impending death, I told myself that didn't matter anymore. My spine was about to be ripped away from my body.

As a last resort, I stabbed the needle into Vess's arm and pressed the plunger. It seemed like a pathetic final act but it was all I had. Maybe the vaccine shot would give him a cold for a few days or something.

He swatted away the syringe as if it were a minor annoyance.

Lucy attacked him, beating on his shoulder with her fists, trying to make him let me go.

He pushed her away with his free hand and she went crashing into the boxes.

I struggled for breath. My fatalism only stretched so far; I would fight for survival up to the last second of my life.

The yellow eyes looked into mine and I realized that this haunting vision was going to be the last thing I ever saw.

Lucy was struggling to regain her feet, screaming, "No!" at Vess. She was crying. I could hear it in her voice but I couldn't see her tears; the only things I could see were those hateful yellow eyes.

Then Vess faltered. His grip on my throat loosened slightly. I fought for breath and managed to suck a little air into my lungs.

Lucy attacked him again, punching him over and over.

Instead of pushing her away, he staggered back a few steps.

And I saw something in those yellow eyes that I had never thought was possible. I saw fear.

He seemed to be weakening. The arm that held me aloft dropped. My feet touched the floor and I tried to push myself away from him. He lost his grip on me and I fell back onto the boxes.

Vess managed to push Lucy away but he looked feeble. Lucy looked like she was readying herself for another attack but stopped when she saw what was happening to Vess.

He leaned against the wall and clutched his arm as if he were having a heart attack. The dark veins that stood out so prominently all over his body seemed to recede. If it wasn't for the blood that covered his naked body, he would look like a normal human being.

I stared in shock. I hadn't expected the vaccine to have such an effect on him.

He looked over at me and the yellowness in his eyes was gone. His eyes were a normal brown color. He looked confused and scared.

"What's happening to me?" he groaned.

Then the eyes widened and his mouth went slack. It was then that I noticed the four bullet holes in his body. They began bleeding, Vess's own blood adding to the blood of those he had killed earlier.

He dropped to the floor as if he had just been shot.

There was no mistaking the way he had fallen and the slackness of his body.

He was dead.

CHAPTER 31

I DIDN'T KNOW IF THE vaccine had killed him or if the cause of death was the group of bullets that were obviously lodged in his body. Maybe the virus had protected him from the damage somehow and now it couldn't because it had been overwhelmed by the vaccine. Johnny Drake had fired at Vess at Site Alpha Two. At the time, we had thought that Vess had dodged the bullet. But maybe Johnny's bullet was the one that had killed Vess a moment ago.

I liked the thought of that.

Jax hadn't moved. She stood looking at Vess's dead body. Then she looked at me and took a step forward. I took another syringe out of my pocket. She hesitated.

Behind her, at the door, Sam and Tanya appeared, brandishing M16s.

"Get down!" Tanya shouted. Lucy and I flatted ourselves to the floor so she and Sam could open fire on Jax.

But Jax leaped through the frosted glass window to the compound outside. Sam and Tanya adjusted their positions and began shooting.

A few seconds later, they ceased fire.

"She got away," Sam said. "Fuck, she's fast."

They saw Vess's dead body lying on the floor.

Sam's eyes went wide. "What the hell?"

"I gave Vess a shot of vaccine," I said. "He turned human. I think the virus had been protecting his body from all the bullets he's taken. When the virus died, the bullet wounds killed him." I rubbed my throat. It hurt to speak. If Vess had applied any more pressure on my windpipe, or if it had lasted any longer, I'd be dead now as well, lying there next to him.

Sam kneeled down to take a closer look at the blood-covered body. "That's some fucked-up shit, man."

"Yeah," Lucy said.

Tanya went over to the broken window and looked out through the shattered glass. "What do you think Jax will do now?"

She'll either come back and try to destroy the vaccine again," Lucy said, "or she'll run." She thought for a moment and then added, "I think she'll run. This vaccine can destroy the virus within her. Since her ultimate goal is to spread the virus, she won't risk meeting the same fate as

Vess. She'll find a place where she can infect as many people as possible before the vaccine is widely distributed."

"Yeah, that sounds most likely," Tanya said. "At least when we catch up with her, we'll know how to kill her." Her voice was tinged with sadness.

I put a hand on her shoulder. "At least she didn't end up as one of the military's experiments."

She nodded.

"Speaking of military experiments," Sam said, "we shouldn't leave Vess's body here for those fuckers to dissect."

He was right. After what the brigadier had said about the government wanting to experiment on a Type 1, it would be dangerous to leave the body here. Vess looked totally human in death but who knew what the military scientists might discover if they examined the body at a cellular level?

I checked the situation outside. There was no one around; the soldiers were still busy with the hybrids. Gunshots and shouts drifted down to this end of the camp on the breeze.

"Let's get it in the bus," I said.

Sam lifted Vess's head and shoulders off the floor. I took the feet and we made our way out of the hut. Tanya and Lucy stayed behind with the M16s just in case Jax came back, and Tanya reloaded my Walther with a fresh magazine in case Sam and I met her on our way to the bus.

I kept an eye out as we moved across the compound, but I was sure Jax had fled.

Vess's flesh was slick with blood, making his corpse more difficult to carry. We managed to get it into the bus and lay it beneath the back seats, out of sight. Then we went into the washrooms and cleaned our hands before heading back to the girls.

By the time all four of us were heading back to the bus, some of the soldiers were returning from the northern quadrant. They looked upset and downcast. I wondered how many of their number had been lost in the hybrid attack.

Captain Price came over to us. His face was set into a hard mask of determination but there were tears in his eyes. "Some of the hybrids were the men that went missing from this camp," he said. "It's one thing to fight an unknown enemy but when you have to kill someone you used to know, it's a damned terrible business."

I nodded. We all knew the heart-wrenching consequences of having our friends become enemies.

The brigadier came marching up to us angrily. "What the bloody hell has happened here?"

"I told you what was going to happen," I said. "I warned you. You wouldn't listen."

He came up to me, putting his face close to mine and pointing at me. "If you let her go, I'll have you court-martialed!"

"Of course we didn't let her go," I said. "She did that all by herself. Your men are lying dead back there because of your arrogance."

"You're all going to jail," he said. "What you did amounts to treason."

I'd heard enough of his bullshit. I hit him. He stumbled backward and fell to the ground, holding his nose as it began to pour blood.

The soldiers around us looked shocked. They didn't know what to do. Two of them helped the brigadier to his feet.

"Arrest them," he shouted, pointing at us. "Take them into custody."

The soldiers moved forward. Tanya and Lucy leveled the M16s at them. The soldiers halted.

"You won't be taking us anywhere," I said.

We moved backward to the bus, the girls keeping their guns trained on the soldiers.

As soon as we climbed aboard, Sam started the engine and reversed through the main gate, knocking it down. He kept the bus in reverse all the way to the motorway, where he maneuvered us into position to drive back along it to get to the roads that would take us to the coast.

"Are they following us?" I asked nervously as we drove along the center lane. If the convoy of armed Jeeps came after us, we stood no chance in a bus.

"No," Sam said, checking the mirror.

"I don't think the brigadier's hatred of us has spread to the other soldiers," Tanya said.

"Wait a minute," Sam said. "There's a Jeep following us."

I looked through the rear window. A single Jeep was on our tail, with a driver, a passenger, and a soldier manning the mounted gun.

"It's only one Jeep," Tanya said.

I sighed. "That's all they need to blow this bus to hell."

The Jeep came up behind us fast. Tanya and Lucy prepared the M16s but I had a feeling they weren't going to get a chance to use them. We'd seen how efficiently the mounted guns had dealt with the bandits.

The Jeep raced up alongside us. It was Captain Price in the passenger seat. He motioned to Sam to stop.

"What do I do?" Sam asked.

"You might as well stop," I said.

He brought us to a complete stop. The Jeep stayed next to us. Price jumped out and knocked on the bus door. Sam opened it. The door opened with a hydraulic hiss.

Price came on board. He stood at the front of the aisle between the seats as if he were a tour guide about to point out the local landmarks. "The brigadier has sent me to bring you back to the camp."

"I'll tell you now, that isn't going to happen," Tanya said. She and Lucy had their guns pointed at Price.

"No, it isn't," he agreed. "There's no need for the weapons. I'm not taking you anywhere. You'll have to excuse the brigadier; he's a military man through and through. Doesn't believe civilians have much value, even though it's them he's supposed to be fighting for.

"You people don't belong in jail. You're doing just as much good out here as we are, maybe even more. We're bound by rules and regulations. Sometimes they get in the way.

"So, as I said, I came after you as per the brigadier's orders but you were already gone when I got to the motorway."

"Thanks," Sam said, "but why did you have to stop us just to tell us that? I mean, it's nice that you want to say goodbye and everything, but we'd have gotten over our heartbreak if you'd just let us leave without saying a word. We wouldn't have looked back, man."

"I came to tell you that you may have underestimated the brigadier. He knows you killed something in Lab 3. We found the bloodstain on the floor and a trail leading to where this bus was parked. He thinks you killed your friend Jax and removed the body so the scientists can't examine it."

We said nothing. Price studied our faces, then nodded and gave a signal to the gunner in the Jeep. The gunner jumped down onto the road, took something from the vehicle and brought it around to the open bus door. He handed it to Price.

It was a shovel.

Price tossed it down into the aisle. The shovel clattered on the floor of the bus.

"Make sure you bury it deep," he said.

With that, he exited the bus and went back to his Jeep. He gave us a slight nod before the Jeep turned and headed back to Camp Prometheus.

"Wow," Sam said.

I picked up the shovel and placed it on the back seat. Even though he worked for the military, Price must have the same trepidation as us when it came to letting them study the body of a Type 1 for weaponization purposes.

"We'll bury the body on the cliffs," Tanya said. "Let's go, Sam."

He nodded and got us moving.

I hoped the short drive to the coast was going to be uneventful. We had a body to bury and I finally had a location for Joe and my parents.

I took the slip of paper out of my pocket and read it over and over, feeling as if I might be in a dream.

Tomorrow, I was going to see my family.

CHAPTER 32

WE PARKED THE BUS BY the cafe and climbed out into the afternoon sun. The *Easy* and the *Escape* waited on a gently rolling sea. I wanted to get the burial over as soon as possible and return to the comfort of the boat.

Across the road, a small stone wall marked the edge of a field. It looked as good a place as any to dispose of Vess's body A lone elm tree stood in the field. With shovel in hand, Sam vaulted over the wall and began digging in the shade beneath the tree.

When he had a grave deep enough, he came back and said, "All ready." We struggled to get the body over the wall but finally managed to carry it across the field and into the grave. Price had said to bury the body deep, and Sam had dug a hole that would suffice. We rolled Vess in.

"Tell me something," Sam said. "Are we burying the body out of respect or just to hide it?"

"Just to hide it," I said.

We filled in the hole quickly. As we climbed over the wall and back onto the road, I looked back. No one would ever suspect that patient zero was buried beneath that tree.

Tanya grabbed the magpie from the bus and we descended the steps to the beach. The Zodiac was exactly where we had left it among the rocks.

We had driven here without incident, buried the body without being seen, and found the Zodiac with no trouble. Maybe our luck was changing for the better.

As we launched the small craft, I heard the low buzz of a drone overhead. The magpie sat by Tanya's feet. We were safe.

* * *

We sailed out from the coast and turned the boats south. Our destination was Camp Achilles in Wales. We would go ashore tomorrow. For now, we wanted to get the boats near enough to Swansea Marina to assess the situation there. The last time we had been there, it had been crawling with soldiers and military vehicles. That shouldn't be a problem now that we had the ID badges that said we worked for the MoD but we didn't want to blunder into an area where the army had a "shoot first, ask questions later" policy.

If we saw a large military presence, we would find another place to go ashore.

When we arrived at the marina, our luck seemed to be holding out; the place was deserted. Tanya's voice came over the radio. "Alex, where are the soldiers we saw last time?"

"I guess they don't need them here now that the drones are patrolling," I suggested. It made sense to me that if they had drones flying along the coastline, any soldiers on the ground would be redundant and better utilized elsewhere.

"We'll land there tomorrow, then," Tanya said. "Got anything good for dinner?"

I smiled. It felt good to deal with something as mundane as what was on tonight's dinner menu. "We've got some burgers."

"Sounds good. We'll be over soon."

The rest of the evening passed pleasantly and quickly. We all felt a sense of accomplishment. Despite numerous setbacks, we had delivered the first batch of vaccine. Marilyn MacDonald was going to have to find someone else to deliver the subsequent batches because, even if we wanted to help with that, we weren't welcome at Camp Prometheus anymore. As far as Operation Wildfire was concerned, we were done.

That night, I dreamed of my family living on board the *Easy* with us, safe from the horrors on the mainland. With Joe on board, I could relax a little and spend time with

Lucy while my brother piloted the boat. Joe always made me feel safe, no matter what.

I woke up in the night but this time it wasn't because I'd had a nightmare; I just needed the bathroom. When that was done, I sat up in bed listening to the sea and Lucy's deep, relaxed breathing.

Through the porthole, I could see the calm night. The moon cast a silver shimmer over the water.

If everything went well, my family would be on the boat tomorrow. I could hardly wait to show them around the *Easy*.

Everything was going to be perfect.

CHAPTER 33

T HE NEXT MORNING, SAM AND I took the Zodiac to Swansea Marina and found a Ford Focus parked near the marine goods store. Sam broke into the car and hot-wired it. We put the magpie on the back seat and drove inland.

Lucy and Tanya stayed on the boats because we had to make sure we had enough room in whatever vehicle we took to drive my parents and Joe back to the marina.

Despite the calm and clear night, the morning had brought storm clouds and rain. As we drove along the main road that led to the mountains, Sam turned on the wipers and headlights. "Today's the day, dude," he said, seeming genuinely pleased for me. "You get to introduce us to your parents."

I grinned. I felt full of nervous energy. How much would Joe and my parents have changed? How much would they think I'd changed?

Camp Achilles wasn't far from the coast. We couldn't miss it because there were red signs everywhere pointing to its location. It was nestled between two mountains, surrounded by the same wire fence and guard towers we had seen at the other camps.

At the gate, we presented our ID badges and told them who we were here to see. The guards waved us through and told us to wait in our car at the parking area.

We did, and the rain streamed over the windows, obscuring our view of the camp.

"It's a good thing we have these badges," Sam said. "They wouldn't let just anybody come into a camp and take people out of it."

"I know," I said. The army's objective was to get as many people into the camps as possible, not let them leave. My badge meant I could take my family out of Achilles and no one would bat an eyelid. My luck was still holding out.

A soldier dressed in a green rain slicker knocked on the window and beckoned us to follow him. Sam stayed in the car while the soldier led me to a hut that was simply called Hut 4. Very imaginative.

He opened the door and held it open while I entered. The room was bare. I guessed that Hut 4 had many different uses and was furnished for whatever need it was being used for at the time. A man visiting his family didn't require any furnishing at all.

A second door opened and my heart leaped as my dad stepped through it and into the room. He saw me and rushed forward to hug me. That hug felt so good. I couldn't remember the last time I had hugged my dad.

"Alex," he said, holding me tight. "My boy is alive. We thought you were dead."

"I'm fine, Dad."

He held me at arm's length. "You're more than fine. Look at you. You've lost weight. And you look stronger. Much stronger."

His face fell a little and he said, "I wish your mother could see you now."

I felt a slight panic rush through me. "You mean she can't? Where is she?" I looked at the door he had entered through. "Isn't she here?"

"Joe is here," he said. "He'll be along shortly. Your mother..." His voice trailed off and he shook his head.

"What? Dad, how? What happened?" I felt numb. My mother couldn't be dead, she just couldn't.

"It was when we moved here from the other camp. We were attacked on the road. A lot of people didn't make it."

I couldn't believe it. "When?"

"Two weeks ago." He looked at me with tears spilling down his cheeks. "I miss her, Alex." We hugged again, only this time it was because he needed physical support and I was giving it to him.

231

The door opened and Joe walked in. When he saw me, his face lit up. "Alex!" He came over and put his arms around me and Dad.

"We didn't know you were alive," he said. "You look great."

I smiled. Unfortunately, I couldn't return the compliment. Both Joe and my dad looked pale and drawn. There was something about their slumped postures and dull eyes that made me feel like they had both given up on life. If I had to describe them in one word, that word would be "defeated".

But that would change. A few days at sea would lift their spirits. A new life away from this place would bring back the father and brother I knew.

"I've got a boat," I said. "You can come with me and leave this place behind. I've got friends. You'll really like them. And we…"

"No," my dad said. "We can't leave here, Alex."

"Yes, you can. It's okay. I've got a badge that gives me some authority. I can…"

"No, Alex," Joe said. "Dad didn't mean it that way. He meant that we can't leave here because this is the only place we're safe."

"What?" I felt confused. Didn't they realize that I had survived all this time without being in a camp?

"It's dangerous out there," Joe said. "We've been on the road. People got killed. We're not doing it again. They look after us here."

I couldn't believe what I was hearing. Joe had always been the brave one, the brother I looked up to. I'd always wanted to be like him. Now he was acting as if he were afraid of his own shadow.

"I'm not saying it isn't dangerous," I said. "Of course it's dangerous. But we live on a boat. We're not confined in a camp. We're free. Surely you can see that life is better than living like caged animals."

Dad shook his head. "We've seen what's out there. Those monsters. We don't want to see anything like that again."

They reminded me of the people hiding at the motorway services. But these two men weren't strangers, they were my family. I never expected them to be like this.

"You reached out to me on the radio," I said. "You wanted to be with me."

"Of course we did," Joe said. "We wanted you to come to the camp. We wanted to know that you were safe."

"I am safe, and I don't need a camp," I said, suddenly angry. Why the hell did they want to live under the army's rule instead of being free? It didn't make any sense to me. I could never give up my liberty like that.

"It's not so bad," Dad said. "We get food and water and we're protected. Come and live with us, Alex. The army will keep us all safe until this mess blows over. Then we can go home."

Was this the garbage they were being told by the authorities? "This situation isn't going to just blow over.

Nothing will ever be the same again. There are things we can do to try and make things better but sitting in a camp and putting our heads in the sand isn't one of them. We need to fight. If we're ever going to beat the undead, we need to destroy them."

"No," Joe said, shaking his head. "There are people paid to do that. Trained soldiers. It isn't up to us."

"What happened to you, Joe? You used to be strong. I was the one who always needed protecting and you were there to do it. But now, it's like you've given up."

"There are some things we can't fight," he said.

"Come with me to the boat," I said. "Both of you. You'll see that we don't have to give up and let the undead take over."

I reached out for Joe and he shrank back as if he were afraid of me. That was when I realized I was wasting my time here. Dad and Joe had lost whatever spirit they had once possessed. Whether it was the death of my mother or simply the gravity of the undead situation, something had broken them.

"I have to go," I said.

"No, Alex, stay," Dad said. "I'll worry about you if you go out there."

I looked at them both and said, "Worry about yourself."

I turned to leave. I knew they were safe for the moment but there was nothing I could do to help them further.

Except one thing. I took the two syringes from my pocket and handed them to my father. "These contain a vaccine that protects you from being turned if you're bitten. I brought them for you."

He looked down at the syringes in his hand and then handed them back to me. "We don't need these. We're safe here."

I didn't argue. They were in total denial of what was going on around them if they thought they were 100% safe.

I put the syringes back into my pocket. "Goodbye." I walked out into the rain and over to the car. When I slid into the passenger seat, my face was wet with rain and tears.

"Hey, man, where are your folks?" Sam asked.

"They're staying here," I said.

"Okay," he said. He started the car and drove toward the gate. As we drove through it and onto the road beyond, I looked back at the camp with its wire fence and guard towers. After what I had seen Jax and Vess do at Prometheus, Camp Achilles looked vulnerable.

Sam didn't say anything during the drive back to Swansea. He might be loud and brash sometimes but when it mattered, like now, he knew when to keep quiet.

I just sat, looking at the road ahead and thinking about the people I knew who had died in this apocalypse: Mike, Elena, Johnny, Jax. And now I could add Joe and my father to that list.

They might still be breathing, but they were already dead inside.

* * *

We spent the rest of the day taking the boats out into deeper water. I told the others about my father and brother and the fate of my mother. Everyone was sympathetic but I didn't want their sympathy, only their friendship. We put Survivor Radio on and fished off the aft deck and played cards in the living area.

When night fell, the rain stopped. I stepped out onto the foredeck and stared up at the bright stars and silver moon. My thoughts were unfocused. I felt adrift like the boat.

Lucy came out and snuggled close to me in the evening chill. "Are you okay, Alex?"

"Yeah, I'm fine. It was a shock seeing how much my dad and Joe had changed, and learning about the death of my mother. In a way, I wish I hadn't found them. At least that way, I'd remember them how they were. I'd have some hope that my mother was still alive."

We stood together in silence for a while, enjoying the physical closeness we shared.

It was Lucy who broke the silence. "What are we going to do now?" she asked.

"We'll do what we've always done," I said. "At one time, my dream was to put all this behind us and just keep

236

sailing. But today, I told my dad and brother that we have to keep fighting the undead. And I was right. I can't turn my back and sail away while there's still fighting to be done."

"So we fight," she said.

"Yeah," I said, holding her close and watching the dark coastline. "We fight."

CHAPTER 34

Two Days Later

RIGADIER GORDON HATED FLYING. As the Chinook dropped out of the sky to the parking lot below, he felt his stomach lurch. Still, even though his insides were churning, he ensured that his outward appearance remained calm. No need to let his men see his weakness.

The Chinook, which had flown from an Air Force base specifically to fly Gordon on this mission when he told them of its importance, touched the ground and he let out a mental sigh of relief. He exited the chopper first, as befitted his rank, but did not rush. Once his feet were on the asphalt parking lot, he felt much better.

This was definitely the correct location. The bus was parked exactly where the drone operator had said it was.

The dozen guards he had brought with him assumed firing positions around the Chinook, near the bus, and on the road.

Gordon put his hands on his hips and surveyed the area. The run-down cafe looked like a possible hiding place for nasties but he hoped they wouldn't be here long enough to have to worry about that.

If Price had done his job properly and stopped the damned bus on the motorway like he was supposed to, Gordon wouldn't have had to contact the drone operators and tell them to watch the coast for the vehicle, those four miscreants wouldn't have buried the Type 1's body beneath the elm tree in the field across the road, and Gordon wouldn't be here now.

He could have stayed at the camp, of course, and simply sent the men to recover the body, but after Price had let him down, he felt the need to supervise this operation himself.

Two lance corporals he had tasked to dig up the body joined him as he crossed the road. Each man held a shovel.

Gordon halted at the edge of the road and stood with his hands clasped behind his back. "Under that tree," he told them.

They hurried over the wall and to the tree in double time.

Gordon turned and looked out to sea. It was a clear day and the sea was calm, almost like blue glass.

Forty minutes later, he saw the lance corporals pull something out of the ground. He waited patiently while they carried it across the field and heaved it over the wall. They laid it at Gordon's feet.

When he saw the body, he frowned.

It was the body of a man.

"Who is this?" he asked the two men. "Is he one of ours?"

"I don't think so, Sir," one of them replied.

What the bloody hell were those four survivors playing at? Had they guessed that he would access the drones, and switched the body of the woman they called Jax for this unknown man? The victory he had felt at outsmarting those hooligans faded when he realized he might have been outsmarted himself.

No, there was no way they would go to the trouble of burying a body that was unimportant. There was something more going on here than met the eye.

"Right," he told the lance corporals. "Get this in the chopper. I want the scientists to have a look at it."

"Yes, Sir," they said in unison. They picked up the body and hurried to the Chinook.

Gordon followed them at a leisurely pace, not wanting to get on board the damned chopper just yet.

Ten minutes later, he could hesitate no longer. He ordered the guards onto the Chinook and strapped himself into his seat. He looked over at the body, which was now wrapped in a blanket and lying at the rear of the aircraft.

He was going to order a full investigation of that corpse in the lab.

If it held any secrets, it would soon give them up to the scientists.

EPILOGUE

Two Weeks Later

New York Harbor, New York

OFFICER GARY RAMIREZ STEPPED OUT of his patrol car and into the cold night air. He'd been about to finish his shift and go home when he'd received the call telling him to get his ass to the docks. Someone had called in a disturbance and he was the closest unit.

He didn't really mind that he was going home late. It wasn't as if there was anyone there waiting for him.

It had been almost two months since Lydia had gone and ever since the day she'd walked out, most of his evenings were lost to binge-watching cop shows on TV, during which he would laugh at the inconsistencies between real cop work and TV cop work, and binge-drinking Coors, during which he would eventually pass out.

Everything looked quiet at the docks. Ramirez made his way between the shipping crates, wondering where the stevedores were. Every other time he had come down here, the place had been bustling with activity. Now, it was dead.

He could see ships and hear activity in other areas of the harbor but the area he was standing in, the area where someone had called in a disturbance, was as quiet as the grave.

Disturbance my ass, he thought. Probably a crank call.

But the hairs on the back of his neck were rising, as if there was something here that he was sensing but not seeing.

He suddenly wanted to return to his car. A night of TV cop shows and Coors held more appeal right now than it had a couple of minutes ago.

"Don't get spooked," he told himself.

He drew his gun, a Glock 19, from its holster and decided to proceed along the dock despite the fear that was gnawing at his gut.

He saw a boat that looked like it had crashed into the dock up ahead. The craft was listing to one side and its hull was torn open. Was this the disturbance someone had called in? A crashed boat?

Ramirez walked up to the vessel and admired it. This was the type of boat that belonged to rich families who spent their weekends cruising on the Atlantic. He checked the name painted on the hull in swirling black and gold letters. *The Broken Promise*.

He looked around. The dock was deserted so who the hell had called 911 about a disturbance?

"Hello?' he called out. "Is anyone on board?"

No answer. He shook his head. This was crazy. Where was the Port Authority? Wasn't this their problem?

Should he go on board and check it out?

He stood, looking at the boat, undecided about what to do. Maybe he should call for backup. But if this turned out to be nothing but a damaged boat, the guys at the station would never let him live it down.

He was about to step onto *The Broken Promise* when he heard a noise behind him. He whirled around, Glock coming up to firing position. He saw a figure running between the shipping crates. Ramirez had to blink twice to make sure he wasn't seeing things because he was sure it had been a naked woman.

"Really?' he asked himself. "Did I really just see a naked woman running along the dock?" Hell, why not? He had seen crazier things during his thirteen years on the force.

She looked like she was covered in tattoos. Some sort of dark vine design, maybe.

Where had she come from?

Leaving the boat, he walked back along the dock to where the woman had appeared. A warehouse door was open. Ramirez took his flashlight and shone it into the darkness beyond the doorway.

He saw many faces staring back at him.

And all of them had hateful yellow eyes.

Stay informed of new releases by joining the mailing list:
http://eepurl.com/OKFY9

Want to contact the author?
shaunharbinger@gmail.com

Printed in Great Britain
by Amazon

59224721R00151